If I Could Be Like Jennifer Taylor

Barbara Ehrentreu

IF I COULD BE LIKE JENNIFER TAYLOR

◆

BARBARA EHRENTREU

Dedication

I dedicate this to Paula Danziger for her inspiration and support.

Acknowledgements

This book began in Paula Danziger's writing workshop. Thank you to YA-authors: Jody Feldman, Lynn Fazenbaker, Cynthia Lord, Claudia Pearson, Greg Fishbone, Meghan McCarthy, Tracy Hurley who read my first draft and helped me with their comments. A big thank you to Kathy Helmer, who was my beta reader. Thank you to the members of KidsMuse who also helped me. Another thank you to Laura Backes and Linda Arms White for their excellent help during Children's Author's Bootcamp. A heartfelt thank you to my daughter, Rachel, who was always there when I needed her and helped me with my blurb. Finally, thank you to my editors, Nancy Bell and Penny Ehrenkranz, and to my daughter, Rachel, who was always there when needed. And lastly, I want to thank my daughter Sara for being the inspiration for both of the characters of Carolyn and Jennifer.

Contents

Dedication 4

Acknowledgements 5

Contents 6

Chapter One 8

Chapter Two 11

Chapter Three 19

Chapter Four 23

Chapter Five 33

Chapter Six.. 37

Chapter Seven.. 44

Chapter Eight 55

Chapter Nine 64

Chapter Ten 70

Chapter Eleven.. 80

Chapter Twelve 94

Chapter Thirteen 110

Chapter Fourteen 115

Chapter Fifteen...122

Chapter Sixteen 130

Chapter Seventeen 138

Chapter Eighteen 145

Chapter Nineteen...151

Chapter Twenty...156

Chapter Twenty-One..159

Chapter Twenty-Two 168

Chapter Twenty-Three..176

Chapter Twenty-Four..181

Chapter Twenty-Five..187

Chapter Twenty-Six...193

Chapter Twenty-Seven 198

Chapter Twenty-Eight..201

Chapter Twenty-Nine...204

Chapter Thirty 212

About the Author 221

Chapter 1 222

Chapter One

I spot him walking toward my locker with a small box in one hand and a plastic fork in the other. My Crush! He hands me the box, and I open it. Inside is a piece of luscious chocolate cake with chocolate frosting. I look up into his blue eyes and give him the box so I can touch his cheek as I smooth his dark hair.

"You always know just what I like."

He smiles and feeds me a forkful of cake. I don't have to worry about eating it because I can eat anything I want and not gain weight. He places the cake box in my locker so he can put his arms around me.

The first bell rings in my ears. I ignore it because I'm thin and blonde and floating in the arms of my dark-haired crush. The other cheerleaders run up to us laughing and kidding around, and I'm about to speak. The ringing gets louder.

The dream evaporates, and I realize it's the darn alarm piercing my sleep. Slamming my fist onto the snooze button, I get this nagging feeling. Then I remember. I have something to do. . *Worse luck, I have to do it, not as the slender blonde beauty in my dream, but as the real Carolyn Samuels with my brown curly hair hanging like shriveled spaghetti, mud brown eyes, and a body too large for fashion.*

I see my new book bag is packed and ready by the door with the initials C. S. in blue, my favorite color. Suddenly it hits me, and I get this dizzy let-me-plop-on-the-pillow feeling. Freshman year of high school—first day. My brain is ready, but my body isn't. Jennifer will be there. Math class and Jennifer; gym class with Jennifer. My body curls into a fetal position, and I throw the covers over my head. Don't faint Carolyn, I tell myself, panting.

Dangling over the chair are those size twelve jeans, clown pants—hardly a fashion statement. I groan. Paired with the red long-sleeved T-shirt, they looked so good on the mannequin; I'll look like a stoplight. What was I thinking? How could I possibly go to school looking like such a freak?

Actually, the real reason I can't go is Jennifer, with her long straight blonde hair, perfect body, and clothes from magazines like *Teen* and *Seventeen.*

Yuck. I feel sick, sick with Jenniferitis.

I hear Mom's footsteps on the stairs.

"Why are you still in bed?" She comes upstairs and peeks into my room with a puzzled look on her face.

Moving the blanket up to my nose, I say, "Mom, I can't stop shivering, and my stomach and head hurt."

She feels my head and looks at me with mothervision. "Carolyn, did you think I'd fall for your tricks?"

I cringe. Now my stomach and head ache for real. Defeated, I climb out of bed and get washed. I slip the hated outfit onto my body and glance at my bloated reflection in the mirror. It's too late to change. I'm stuck with this. If only I could be like Jennifer Taylor.

After picking up my book bag, I race down the stairs, take a couple of bites of a chocolate-chocolate chip muffin and a few sips of non-fat milk. I almost trip over a lump blocking the door. Max, our five-year old Newfoundland raises his massive bear-like head, sniffing like he's never eaten a thing in his life when he sees my muffin. I glance at his empty bowl and throw the rest of the muffin into it. He sees it and licks my face; now I'm going to smell like dog food all day. Grabbing a paper towel, I wipe my face and lean to ruffle his soft fur. At least Max doesn't care what I wear. Feed him and rub him under his chin, and he'll cover you with slurpy kisses.

Mom is already in our three-year-old silver Malibu that, like my jeans, doesn't quite make a fashion statement.

On the drive to school, I'm looking forward to seeing Becky and Janie my two best friends from forever. Don't want to see Jennifer's face on the first day of high school.

Chapter Two

Mom barely stops long enough for me to get out of the car before taking her foot off the brake. The car rolls forward. She's late for work. I walk to the grass on the driver's side to escape the clog of first day of school traffic.

"Carolyn, do you have lunch money?" Mom shouts out her window as she passes.

"Yes, Mom. Aren't you going to be late?" I back away from the car.

"Knock 'em dead." Mom uses Dad's dumb expression for luck. The first bell rings, and I wave goodbye. My stomach feels like jelly.

Cutting across the grass, I get to the front door at the same time as Becky and Janie. We smile and start talking all at once on the way to the freshman lockers.

"Becky, I almost didn't come to school today."

"What a shock, as if you don't have this problem every year?" She gives me a smile as she reminds me and pushes away a stray lock of her long auburn hair she's twisted in a bun close to her head. Becky is a dancer, so she wears her hair up most of the time. But the thing about her is, she doesn't care what she wears, even though she could wear almost anything and look terrific.

"Couldn't face my clothes." I open my locker door. "Too bad those jeans we tried on in Norman's made me look like a blimp." The next words almost make me cry, so I practically whisper them. "I'll never lose weight."

"Carolyn, you look great. We all decided not to buy the tighter ones, remember? We wanted to breathe on the first day of school," Becky reassures me, as she looks me up and down. She has the clearest blue eyes.

"Guess that's why we're friends. We like the same clothes and other things," Janie says, tosses her chestnut hair and glances toward the crowd in the hallway near our lockers.

"By other things do you mean Brad?" Becky winks.

"Is he here?" I look frantically in my book bag for my locker mirror and when I find it, check to see if Jennifer is there. She used to hang out with him and his crowd all last year. Jennifer Taylor, the only girl in middle school to go out with a high school guy. No Jennifer. I let out my breath.

We stash our books in our lockers. The hallway has that first day of school smell: fresh paint and floor wax. Combined with the perfume and aftershave worn by everyone, the smell almost suffocates me. One good thing—I haven't seen Jennifer.

I pray I get to class without running into her. I take a breath and step into the wave of traffic with Becky and Janie. Wouldn't you know it? My stomach does a double flip. Jennifer Taylor is a few feet in front of me walking with her best friend Maura.

A big crowd surrounds them, and most of the people in it are staring at the two of them like they're celebrities on a red carpet.

"Jen, that outfit looks amazing on you," Maura, says.

"Yes, well I wanted to wear the outfit I bought in this boutique in Florida, but Mom put her foot down. She said I couldn't show so much skin. It only covers half of my belly, but the over-sweater covers it all."

"Jen, I never saw that one. Remember, we didn't see each other, even to go shopping."

"Yeah, sorry about that, we just got back this weekend, and Mom made me go shopping with her. Anyway, I had to run over yesterday and buy the only thing they had left. Lucky I'm a size two. But you know, I'm going to wear the outfit I got in Florida next time I go out with Brad. I'll get my belly button pierced even though the witch says no."

Maura says, "If anyone can do it, you can."

Jennifer's wearing the same outfit as I am, but on her, it looks like it did on the mannequin.

She stops in front of my math class, says goodbye to Maura, and stands in the hallway facing away from the door.

I feel like last night's leftovers and hide behind some tall kids so she won't see me. It'll be another year of "Miss Perfect" in my class. Why did I have to be good in math? We're always together in math, and this year it's an advanced class, Honors Math.

I hate Jennifer, the way she talks, and the attention she gets. Most of all, I hate how much I want to be like her. Who wouldn't? Her family owns half of our town. Boys stare at her all the time. She was the first one in middle school to start dating. Worse, she's smart, too. I try not to think what a bitch she is because it might come out of my mouth. Jennifer's right behind me, and what if she heard me? My mind doesn't even want to go there. I pop a breath mint into my mouth for safety. Bad breath is the kiss of death in a crowd of kids.

The bell rings, and I walk into the room and take a seat. As soon as the teacher starts taking attendance, Jennifer appears, and the second bell rings.

"Sit here, Jen," a chorus of voices interrupts him.

"Young lady, please find a seat. Tell your adoring public you can only sit in one place at a time. Maybe you can move every ten minutes, so everyone can have a turn." Our math teacher doesn't sound like he'll fall for Jennifer Taylor's charms. I want to applaud him, but that would be weird, and I'd be labeled all year as the stupid girl who clapped for the teacher on the first day of school.

The whole class laughs, and Jennifer finds a seat next to the best looking boy in the room, naturally.

I'm feeling invisible, a feeling I know well from years past. People around me are smiling and mouthing hellos while the teacher is taking attendance. Maybe the teacher won't call my name. But he does, and the whole class looks around to see who it is. My voice isn't working so well, so I don't answer. I raise my hand to show I'm there, but luck isn't with me. The teacher doesn't see my hand, and he calls my name again.

"Here," I say in a scratchy voice.

"Ribbit," Jennifer stage whispers to the cute guy. "Who brought a frog to school?"

The whole class smiles, but the teacher is too busy to notice anything. "

Jennifer Taylor," he calls her name, and she answers in a clear voice. Class begins, and the teacher introduces himself as Mr. Armbruster.

The next fifty minutes are a blur. I can't tell you what we did, because on the first day, it's all fill out cards and hand out books. I do remember Mr. Armbruster calling on Jennifer instead of me for a problem I knew, because she raised her hand faster than I did and got the credit. Even in class, she's a star. *Can my day get any worse? How am I going to get through this year?*

Becky and Janie meet me outside of class.

"Oh, my God; like I thought, Jennifer is in my Honors Math class. Ugh."

"Carolyn, she won't remember last year. She's only interested in impressing every boy in the school," Janie says. I look into her soulful hazel eyes, and I can almost believe it's true.

Janie has a little sister. (Sorry, I had to change this for the next books.) so she's always babysitting. Janie's always told me the truth, since the day we first met back in kindergarten when we shared the same clay. Her piece was a cute little dog, but mine looked like a blob. Janie is still way into art, and with her busy life, she doesn't have time to think about what she's wearing.

Becky is about to speak, but the bell rings, and we scurry to class. My treatment in high school seems to be a middle school rerun. How did I expect it to be? I should have stayed in bed this morning. And it is only second period.

At lunch, Becky is sitting alone and holding a place for me. Janie has the one before us on gym days. I'm starving, but I force myself to eat nonfat yogurt. I miss Janie being here with Becky and me. The bell rings for seventh period, and I realize it's time for gym. Becky and I start out together.

"Once more we'll be treated to the Jennifer show. 'Miss Perfect' in her color-coordinated gym outfit and her adoring fans watching as she always manages to get chosen team captain," I complain.

"Do you remember the cheering for her when she did that triple somersault down the mats to start the gymnastics unit last year?" Becky says.

"Yes, and then remember how I went next, and I looked like a turtle on its back. Jennifer looked at me and waved her hands at her sides mimicking my ridiculous position, and I'm rolling around on the mat trying and trying to push my body over. I guess it was funny, now I look back on it." I crack a smile. "But, oh my gosh, talk about embarrassing." *Gym again with Jennifer will be too much for me to bear.* I start breathing a little faster

"Maybe she'll be in another gym class," Becky says.

No way, I think. Gym classes in our school are arranged alphabetically, and of course, Samuels and Taylor would be in the same class. Becky's last name is Roberts. We are always together in gym.

Becky pushes on the door to the lockers, and I steel myself for the show that is Jennifer. Kids are milling around getting ready for gym. The smell of old sneakers and unwashed gym clothes mixes with shampoo. Becky and I can barely hear each other over the sound of the showers and the lockers slamming all around us. At least Becky is there to talk to. Maybe it won't be so bad.

Feeling my old hatred of gym, I glance across the locker room and see Jennifer in red designer shorts and a tight sleeveless shirt to match. She's standing in front of the only mirror in the room turning back and forth.

Becky and I slide into our loose camp shorts and a T-shirt, and once they're on, we race onto the gym floor. Always better to be early for gym the first day. You never knew what kind of teacher you'd have. My athletic ability is zero, so I don't take chances. Once I was a few minutes late, and the gym teacher in middle school made me run around the gym ten times. It took me the whole gym period.

Becky and I sit on the low seats in the bleachers, but Jennifer and her group saunter into the gym and choose the highest seats avoiding the rest of us. Miss Gaylon, the gym teacher introduces herself and gives us a few minutes until the last stragglers come from the locker room. For those few minutes, I almost feel comfortable. My breathing returns to normal. I hear giggles from Jennifer and her group, but I ignore it.

"Maybe it won't be so bad this year, Carolyn." Becky always tries to cheer me up now. This wasn't true a few years ago. I had to cheer her up a lot. Becky's brothers are just turning five, and they're both in kindergarten. Her mom remarried after being divorced for ten years. Becky was just getting used to her new stepfather when her mom got pregnant. I remember how miserable Becky was the first year of middle school when her mom spent so much time with her twin brothers and didn't have enough time to help Becky with her homework. Luckily, Becky's stepfather is a history teacher, so she got very interested in history and current events.

"Right, Becky, and maybe I'll learn to be a gymnast in ten minutes. Reality check, remember last year?"

"Okay, I'm hoping it won't be so bad."

"You mean like the dentist finding you only have one cavity and filling it the same day?"

"You're so lame, Carolyn. Since we're all older, maybe she'll treat us differently. People change over the summer you know."

"Look at her, Becky."

Becky turns to look over at the group at the top of the bleachers and then turns back to look me in the eye. "You know you have to put that stupid day behind you."

I pretend not to know what she's talking about.

"What stupid day?" Like I don't remember every detail.

"The zip line day."

"Oh, *that day*," I say with a combination grimace and smile. "The day I wound up having to climb off the platform. I wanted to bore a hole into the ground so I wouldn't have to walk past them but couldn't, and everyone screamed at me: 'Breathe, Carolyn, breathe.'"

"You have to admit it was funny the way the gym teacher ran up the ladder like a squirrel to rescue you. Everyone laughed at how stupid she looked. Jennifer got the whole class going with that ridiculous 'breathe, Carolyn, breathe.'" Becky looks behind her to Jennifer. "You know I wanted to run over and punch her, but I couldn't because I was still on the platform, and it was my turn to go."

"Yeah, if I had a few more minutes, I would have been able to get up the courage to grip the zip line and hook myself to it. Stupid teacher didn't give me a chance. This not breathing thing when I get nervous really sucks."

Becky nods because she knows me so well.

"So then Jennifer started with that horrible chant, and of course, the whole class followed her, like always." My eyes fill with tears as I remember, and my breathing is getting worse by the minute.

"I thought it was a dumb idea to do ropes course stuff in school. We did it at my camp the summer before, and no one was forced to do it. Anyone could get nervous with Jennifer in front of them," Becky comforts me.

I continue talking as if I'm in a trance. "Remember how last year whenever I ran into Jennifer she would whisper 'breathe, Carolyn, breathe,' so no one could hear it except me. Once she did it just before I had to go up in front of the class in math. Sometimes she would do it in front of everyone and, of course, get a big laugh while I wanted to turn into a piece of furniture."

Becky grabs my arm. "Do we have to go back over this again? You need to forget about it." She takes her hand away from my arm as I continue to speak.

"Becky, I can't. The thing is it's this bad movie in my brain looping the same horrible scenes. The funny thing is, most of the time, she would ignore me. I would never know what she was going to do. You have to admire someone so single-minded she managed to get to me at just the right time. You remember don't you? And today did you see how she wore the same outfit as me? It's spooky."

My funny breathing returns as Miss Gaylon tells us to line up on the yellow line alphabetically. I hope there will be someone to go between Jennifer and me. No luck. Jennifer is going to be behind me all year. I hold my breath. I couldn't stand more of the same this year. I pray for the day to end soon. A glance at my new watch shows me fifteen more minutes left of the period. *Is Miss Gaylon's voice getting lower? What is that pounding in my ears?*

Jennifer turns to face me, and I hear, "Breathe, Carolyn, breathe." Then my world turns black.

Chapter Three

The hard wood floor of the gym is the first thing I see when my eyes open. Gradually my vision clears, and a pair of white and pink leather sneakers appears in front of me. Two hands reach to grab me, but I want to stay on the floor. The hands belong to Jennifer. Before I can pick my head up above shoe level, the entire class crowds around me. Well, I'm not invisible anymore. I have risen to an object of pity. I raise myself to a sitting position in case I feel a little faint. I wouldn't want to faint twice in one gym period. Maybe they'd think I tripped or got pushed. Meanwhile Jennifer is mouthing, "Breathe, Carolyn, breathe," and everyone looks like they remember middle school.

Miss Gaylon has finished her attendance and sees me on the floor. Scanning the attendance sheet, she finds my name. "Carolyn Samuels, what are you doing on the floor?"

"Miss Gaylon, I think she tripped. I noticed her on the floor and helped her up. Isn't that right, Carolyn?" Jennifer says.

"Yes, Miss Gaylon. Jennifer came over and tried to help me, but I feel fine now." Sure, I do, and it doesn't matter the whole room is spinning like a merry-go-round. I want this moment to be over fast.

"Miss Samuels you need to see the nurse. Jennifer please accompany Miss Samuels to the nurse. She doesn't look like she can get there alone." I start to walk to the door, but I am swaying and can't keep straight.

"Yes, Miss Gaylon, I would be happy to take Carolyn."

I can't believe it. Jennifer is taking me to the nurse. This put the icing on the cake.

"Miss Gaylon, since it's almost the end of the period anyway, do I need to come back to class?" Jennifer asks.

"Yes, you need to bring a note back here for me to see. Otherwise I'll have to give you an unexcused absence." Jennifer scowls for a moment then her face brightens.

On the way to the nurse, Jennifer keeps laughing and saying, "Breathe, Carolyn, breathe, and kaboom down you go. I wish I had my phone to capture this Kodak moment. It's priceless; we're standing in line, and you hit the floor. Everyone in school should know about this."

She reaches into the back pocket of her shorts to get her lip-gloss and applies it to her already perfect lips while we are walking.

"Jennifer, you don't have to take me the whole way to the nurse. I feel fine now."

"What if you forget to breathe again, and someone finds you lying in the hallway? Anyway, you gave me the perfect way to get out of gym to see Brad. He gets out of class early for football practice. So come on and don't waste any time."

We get to the nurse's office, which is as chaotic as it gets. Kids are everywhere lying on the brown fake leather beds and sitting on plastic chairs. The nurse's outfit is stained and strands of her hair are hanging over her face. There are people in kitchen staff uniforms there, too. Everyone looks kind of pale and miserable. Some are moaning. The nurse tells me to fill out a form, sit down, and wait. Jennifer gets a note back to class from the nurse's assistant. Kids are mumbling about some kind of food poisoning from the cafeteria food. I'm glad I don't eat that garbage. I live on yogurt, but it doesn't do any good. I don't lose a pound.

"Jennifer," I shout to stop her from walking out of the nurse's office.

She turns around and stares at me like I'm an ant crawling on her leg. "What do you want? I have only a few minutes, and then he has to go. The coach gets angry if they're late."

"I'll do anything for you if you won't tell anyone about my fainting in gym this afternoon. Didn't you have enough fun with me last year?"

She starts walking out of the door, but turns and looks at me with her steel blue eyes. "I need you to do me a favor."

"What do you want?" I picture eating worms or walking naked in the hallway, something totally unspeakable. I'm not ready for her next words.

"I have to go to this ridiculous dinner party tonight with my parents, and I won't be able to get my math homework done. If you do it for me, I'll keep this quiet."

"You'd trust me to do your homework? Why?"

"You've always done well in math, and you'll do a good job. Remember it must be here tomorrow morning before school. Otherwise I'll accidentally tell every freshman I know about today and maybe even a few juniors, too."

"Yes." I did say I'd do anything.

"We'll be even then, and I'll let everyone think you tripped. You're so easy to tease. I'll let you go this time, but that homework is in my hands before class tomorrow or no deal. I'll meet you outside of the school. Gotta go now."

I exhale and realize I've been holding my breath again. Jennifer sees my face and says, "Breathe, Carolyn, breathe." She laughs and walks out of the door. The nurse is really swamped, so I start helping by getting drinks for people, and then the last bell rings. I am literally saved by the bell. The nurse is too busy to see me, and I slip out of the office, get to my gym locker, and see Becky.

"Carolyn, are you okay? I can't believe Jennifer took you to the nurse. Did the nurse see you?"

"No, there were too many people in there. It happened from lunch. I heard someone in the nurse's office say the refrigerator got turned off during the night because of a power failure. Anyone who ate the tuna got food poisoning. Luckily, yogurt doesn't go bad for a while. You're feeling okay, right? I grab Becky's hands and squeeze them. Right now she is my rock. "At least it didn't happen to us. Maybe things are looking up this year." Saying it might make it true.

I can't wait to get home. This day has lasted way longer than it should have. But it isn't over yet. I have two sets of math homework to do, and it has to be perfect. I'm wishing I was invisible again, but if this day is typical of what it's going to be like this year, school and my life won't be like last year at all.

Chapter Four

"In local news, twenty-five high school students and several cafeteria workers became sick today when there was an outbreak of food poisoning at Mill Valley High School. Sources say last night's storm is to blame. The refrigerator was off for seven hours during a power outage, and it affected the tuna salad. Irate parents are meeting tonight. Some are talking about suing the school. Live from Mill Valley High School, this is Danielle Slinka, Fox Five News."

"Dad, why would parents want to sue the school if the electricity went off during the night?" It's after dinner, and we're sitting in the living room watching the local news channel.

"Where did you hear that?"

Didn't he hear it, too? Sometimes with only Dad home, I feel like I'm alone. "Dad, weren't you listening to the news now? Twenty-five kids in my school got food poisoning, and parents are thinking of suing the school."

"Sorry, Carolyn, I wasn't. Ooh, I hope you didn't eat any. I guess we would have known by now, right?" He pretends to get sick and makes the sounds. Uch, my dad can be so gross sometimes.

"No, Dad, I had yogurt, and I'm glad I did. So did Becky."

"Well, the parents are holding the school responsible for their kids getting food poisoning because the school is in *loco parentis*. This means the school is acting like their parents when kids are there. So it's the school's fault they served the tuna fish." Dad is a lawyer, and answers from him are never simple or short.

Dad continues, "How was school today, besides the incident? It was your first day back wasn't it? Mom is sorry she can't be home with you tonight, but she has to work late every night this week. They're in the middle of this big ad campaign, and her boss is making them stay until nine every night. By the time she gets home, you'll probably be in bed. In fact, I'm so tired I'm going upstairs now." He stifles a yawn behind his paper, and I get no chance to answer him.

Mom works at Warner, Biddle, Biddle, and Boone, an advertising agency in the city. We live about a half hour away from New York City in a small town in Westchester. I'm used to her working long hours when she has a big job to do. It would have been better to have her home, especially tonight. I'm not sure I'm doing the right thing copying the homework for Jennifer, but Dad is too sleepy tonight for rational answers. So, I've kind of put myself at the wrong end of a wet floor, and the space is too great to cross. I've got to go through with it.

"Goodnight sweetheart. Oh, I almost forgot, as a special treat, I bought a pint of rocky road ice cream for you." He gives me a kiss on the cheek as I hug him; then he shuffles upstairs one-step at a time. I follow him upstairs, too. It's time to do the homework.

The math homework, which is a review test in our book, is easy stuff, and I think I've aced it. Anyway, I make two copies, and then I do the rest of my homework. I know this isn't middle school. We have homework the first night of school.

Didn't eat my usual two and a half portions at dinner, so I feel hungry, but I'm sick of being too heavy for fashion. I want to look like a lean, sexy dancer in a music video. After my homework is done, I go looking for food. Downstairs the container of rocky road in the freezer is calling me. I ignore it and grab an apple instead. What would it be like to be the right size? Could I be popular? Maybe Jennifer could show me how to be popular. Maybe she could help me learn to tumble so I can try out for cheerleading, my secret passion. The little demon in my head, which won't rest says, *Right Carolyn, and maybe tomorrow you'll be a size four.* Jennifer showing me how to be popular is as likely to happen as Brad becoming my boyfriend. Also, what would Becky and Janie think if I started hanging out with Jennifer? I'd lose my two best friends; no, better to stay in my own tight circle. I get into bed and wonder if tomorrow will be the same as today or worse.

Next morning, I wake up, and the day is a clean sheet of paper. I sing while I'm washing and dressing and zoom downstairs. There's time to eat breakfast while Mom is drinking her coffee—whole grain cereal and nonfat milk. She looks up from her last sip and examines me.

"You look pretty happy this morning. When I got home, you were sleeping, and I didn't want to wake you. How was it?"

"I'm in Honors Math, Janie can't eat lunch with us when there's gym, and high school is totally different from middle school. We had homework on the first night in every subject."

"So, did you like it? Did anything unusual happen? I thought when I dropped you off, I might get a phone call to pick you up early."

"Did you hear about the food poisoning? Lucky I eat yogurt, right Mom?"

"I know all about that. Everyone heard about it at work. I called Dad before I came home to check you were okay and make sure you weren't sick. I guess he didn't tell you I called. I'm talking about anything else out of the ordinary?"

"No, nothing happened." In my head, I'm telling her all about the fainting in gym and the deal with Jennifer about the homework, but what good would it do. She'd only send me to the doctor, and not breathing when you're nervous is not a disease. It's serious but not life threatening, the story of my life. You couldn't give me medicine for it like Mary Murphy who used to freak out and scream at the top of her lungs when anything went wrong. Her mother took her to the doctor, and he gave her this medicine that makes her all dead in the eyes and mouth. On the plus side, she doesn't scream anymore.

We stroll to the car, and before I toss my book bag in the back, I check the homework one more time. I can't wait to see Jennifer today.

When we arrive at school, I feel like a movie star getting out of her limo, because Becky and Janie are waiting in front and open the car door for me.

"What happened yesterday? Becky told me you fell in gym? Why didn't you call me when you got home?" Janie stares at me.

"Shh, I'm trying to keep it quiet. I don't want a repeat of last year. I had so much homework I couldn't think. Sorry, Janie."

"Okay, so what happened? Why did you fall? Becky wouldn't tell me out here."

"Well you remember what happened last year with Jennifer always sneaking up on me? The thought of her in back of me made me faint, and I fell. I don't think anyone knew what happened. Jennifer helped me up and took me to the nurse."

"Jennifer, as in Jennifer Taylor?" Janie's mouth pops open.

"Don't worry; she didn't do it for me. She wanted to get out of class to see Brad. Jennifer is helping me hide the real reason I fainted."

"Weird," Janie says and rolls her eyes.

"We're definitely in the land of the strange," I say, laughing. I've never lied to my friends, and I wonder why I'm doing it now. Actually, I've never done anyone else's homework for them either. High school has barely begun, and I've embarked on a life of crime.

We've gotten to the front door, and I wander over to Jennifer. She's surrounded by her usual groupies and doesn't pay attention to me. I tell Becky and Janie to go ahead of me, and I stand next to Jennifer. I'm invisible again, but I have to give her the homework before math.

"Jennifer, remember that thing we had to do for math?"

"Sure, just a second." Jennifer tells her friends she's got to help me, and before I know it, we're walking toward the freshman lockers together.

"You did it on loose-leaf, right? I don't want to tear it out of your notebook."

"Yes. I've got two copies."

I grab the books I'll need from my bag, stash it in my locker, and we head toward math.

"Okay, when I say three, we'll switch. I'll take out the homework, and then on the count of three again, we'll switch back."

Jennifer counts to three, and in the middle of the hall, we switch books while we're walking. I'm afraid I'll drop one of them but manage to hold onto hers.

"I've got the homework; now we'll switch back. Ready, one, two, three, switch."

Grabbing for the loose leaf, I almost drop it, but Jennifer's lands in her hands perfectly. I hear her open and close the rings. I close my rings, and it's done.

"Wow, that was pretty quick. I'm surprised, Carolyn. Thought you'd botch this for sure." Jennifer strides away from me like she has to catch a bus.

I'm relieved. The switch was way too stressful for me. I'm surprised we did it so smoothly. I look at my perspiring hands. I'm glad it's over with. Now on to math.

Yesterday Mr. Armbruster seated us alphabetically. I forgot about this, because it was at the end of the period. Now Jennifer is in back of me again. Isn't there anyone who has a name who can fit between us?

After we go over the homework, which I've done right, Mr. Armbruster collects it, and Jennifer looks at me. One corner of her mouth goes up in what might be counted as a tiny smile.

Then the guillotine comes down on my head.

"Miss Samuels," Mr. Armbruster says, "you and Miss Taylor will be partners for this assignment."

Assignment? What assignment? I must have been thinking so hard I missed the assignment.

"Would you repeat the assignment, please? I didn't get all of it when you said it the first time," a girl in the third row asks him. I'm saved by another person in class who hasn't been paying attention either.

"Miss Kurtz, you need to pay more attention when I give an assignment. Since this is the first week of school, I will repeat it. But don't expect this to happen next week. I will give all of your assignments before we go over the homework from now on. Today was an exception. Can all of you remember that?"

Most kids nod their heads and some mutter "yeah," or "okay."

Jennifer is raising her hand.

"Mr. Armbruster, do we have to be with our assigned partners? Can we switch?"

"Miss Taylor this is not a game. We can't switch partners. For the next three days, you and your partner are going to survey as many people as you can. Your task is to discover each person's favorite food, compile a list, and once you have surveyed fifty people, tally the scores, and see which foods are the most popular. You will plot your findings on a graph, which you will compare with the statistics of other schools on the Internet. Your data should be complete by Thursday; on Friday we'll work with it in the computer lab."

I swallow and find my mouth is dry. I have to do this with Jennifer? Three days with her? She barely saw I was there when Maura started to talk with her. Now I have to spend time with her doing a class project?

"I'll give you a few minutes now to discuss this with your partner and decide how you want to do this assignment. I am handing out the rubric, so you will know what is expected of you."

I don't know what to do. Jennifer's not moving from her seat, and she isn't looking over at me. I feel like a total jerk. Did I expect her attitude to change in one day? What was I thinking? I have a partner who's not going to speak to me. She's talking with the cute guy next to her. He's paired with Mary Kurtz, the girl who didn't hear the assignment. I guess I'll have to go to Jennifer's desk and talk with her.

I get up from my seat and turn the desk around to face Jennifer. She doesn't expect to see my face and has a blank look on hers. John, the cute guy, looks angry.

"I suppose we have to talk about what we'll do for the project," I say.

"Guess so. Bye, John, it was nice talking with you." Jennifer moves her desk over to mine.

John looks like his dog died.

"Yeah, great talking to you, too. Now I'll have to go see what my partner is doing." "Carolyn, what do you want? I thought I'd try to get out of this somehow. John doesn't like his partner, and I don't particularly like mine, so I thought we'd switch."

"But Mr. Armbruster said no switching. How will you do it?"

"We'll just do it; then make up some excuse later, like one of you got sick or something."

At this moment, Mr. Armbruster walks down our aisle. He comes closer to us.

"Miss Taylor, I heard what you said to Miss Samuels. There will be no switching at all. Do you understand?"

Jennifer lowers her eyes, like maybe this time she might have gone too far.

I didn't want to be Mary's partner, and I pity John. But the period is almost over, and we have to think of something quick, or we won't get anything done. I want to get an A on this, and I know Jennifer does, too.

"Okay, we'll have to get this done at lunchtime. Since I know practically everyone in school, I'll interview them, and you'll write it down. We'll need paper and pens, and do you have a clipboard, Carolyn?"

"No. Do we need one?"

"Of course we do. What if we have to interview someone in the hallway? Where will you write?"

"Do you have one?" I don't think my mom would buy one for me, because we've bought all of my school supplies already. I hope Jennifer has one.

"I don't have one, but I can get it. But for now, we'll have to use a notebook. Today is Tuesday. By Thursday, we'll be done with our survey, and after Friday, I don't plan to speak to you again. This is going to ruin my reputation."

I'm getting that no breathing I'm about to faint feeling again. This is way more stress than I can take. Who wanted to be her friend anyway? When this school assignment is over, we'll go back to normal. I'll be invisible again.

"We'll have to go shopping to get some materials for this project, since I gather you can't get them yourself. Also, I can't be seen with you in that outfit. Where did you get it?" Jennifer gives me a sour pickle look.

"You don't like what I'm wearing?"

"It would be great for five years ago, but you have to dress much cooler to be around me. Don't you have anything better to wear?"

"Nope." I'm wearing baggy jeans and a loose sweatshirt. I realize she's probably right.

"Well, I'll have to find you something. You can't wear any of my clothes, so we'll have to make do with your stuff. I suppose you can come to the mall with me this afternoon. We'll need construction paper, markers, at least two clipboards, and maybe a few other things for our project. Also, while we're at the mall, maybe you'll get a new pair of jeans and a top. If you want, I'll help you pick some out. This way I know you'll at least have one decent thing to wear."

"One decent thing to wear." What is this? Now Jennifer is going to be my personal shopper? Why? This is a school assignment, not some dumb award show. Why is she so preoccupied with clothes?

I'm shaking inside. Jennifer Taylor wants to go shopping with me. I feel like a traitor to my friends. What will they think?

"Can you get out after school? No, I have a better idea. Don't go home by bus. My mom is picking me up, and she'll take us to the mall. Call your mom and tell her you'll be going there. Do you have a credit card?"

Was she being funny? My mom would never let me carry around her credit card. She barely lets me have it any time. I remember she let me use it once when I needed to buy something for a special occasion. We were in the mall, and I had to bring it back to her immediately. Would she let me have it without her? No way. I couldn't go shopping today. Where would I get the money?

"Jennifer, my mom is at work, and if I ask her if I can go shopping, she'll be angry. I don't have any money or a credit card. She won't let me have her credit card without her being right there to make sure she gets it back. She had her handbag stolen once, and the thieves took her credit cards. In a half hour, they spent over five thousand dollars. No, I can't go."

"Do you have any cash?"

"Well, I have about twenty-five dollars saved from babysitting. Maybe I can get a new pair of jeans with that."

"So that's settled. For today, I'll pretend you're wearing a different outfit. Or I might not look at you. Oooh, how can you go out of your house in something so awful?"

I want to say it's all I have to wear. Can I tell her everything in my closet looks exactly like this? I decide to say nothing.

I'm starting to sweat. This conversation is getting way too personal for a schoolroom. I concentrate on getting the bell to ring.

"I'll meet you in the lunchroom. Will you be with those loser friends? Ewww, the fashion disaster triplets." Jennifer goes back to ignoring me.

Jennifer's ordering me around, and I'm going to the mall with her, all because of Mr. Armbruster and his stupid survey. Did I even care about people's favorite food? We've done a similar assignment every year since middle school. Why don't teachers check with each other? What about Jennifer? Did she even eat? I guess I'll have the answer to that one soon. I turn my desk around and finally the bell rings. What will lunchtime be like, I wonder?

Chapter Five

It's not a gym day, so Janie is eating with us. It almost feels like last year when we did everything together. I'm getting lulled into this calm feeling when halfway through my yogurt, Becky and Janie look up over my head. I see an expression I have seen only once before on their faces when all of us got a triple dip ice cream from Nick's the day Jennifer was there with Brad. With a mixture of longing, jealousy, and hatred, they stare behind me. I turn around to see why they're staring and say, "Hi, Jennifer. Did you call your mom? Is it okay for me to ride with you?"

"Yeah. I'll meet you after school in front where my mom picks me up. Don't be late. I've only got a couple of hours after school allotted for you." She moves to leave but turns back to whisper in my ear, "Breathe, Carolyn, breathe. See you after school." Laughing, she goes back to her table.

Becky comes out of statue mode to squeak to me, "Carolyn, tell me this is the same time zone, and I'm still on Earth. Is Jennifer still standing behind you?"

"No, she's gone, and yes, Becky, she and I are going to the mall. It seems I don't have the proper attire for hanging out with her." I grin, but my friends have a dazed expression on their faces.

"Are you a twin of Carolyn?" Janie says.

"Are you really going with Jennifer to the mall this afternoon?" Becky asks.

"Snap out of it; are you okay? Seriously, guys, Jennifer, and I are doing a project together, and we have to get some supplies. While we're there, she's helping me find an outfit to wear so I won't look so pathetic when we do our survey." I answer as if this is the most ordinary thing in the world. "She's practically forced me to come and promised to pay for the supplies, and we have to do the survey for math, or both of us are going to get into a lot of trouble with Mr.

Armbruster. He put us together as partners, and it's got to be done before Friday. I don't know how I'll survive this. You know how all of those clothes she likes will fit me. I'm doomed if I go and destroyed if I don't go. Great choices, huh?"

Becky and Janie sort of nod their heads, and Becky says, "Well, if it's that much of a must-go-or-I'll-fail kind of thing, then I guess you have to go. Doesn't she, Janie?"

Janie pipes in, "Sure, if you must go, you must go. Anyway, you might get to go to the art supply place, which is my favorite place in the whole mall. How will you stand it, though?"

"I'll try to pretend it's all perfectly normal for me to be there. You know I wouldn't go to the mall without you guys unless I absolutely had to. Are we okay?" I hold my breath hoping my friends will understand.

"Sure, do whatever you have to do." Becky pauses and looks me in the eye. "Don't you think her taking you to the mall is just a little bit weird?"

I let out my breath. My last gulp of yogurt suddenly doesn't taste as sweet. Me in the mall with Jennifer Taylor. What was I thinking? Did I have time to catch up with her and tell her I changed my mind? For the first time in my life, I'm not looking forward to the end of the school day.

The whole afternoon I keep thinking about going to the mall with Jennifer. Then a thought pops into my head. Will Brad be there? How will I talk to him? I think of Brad, and my insides churn. He's my not-so-secret crush. At least not to Becky and Janie, and they would hold my secrets no matter what. When he was an eighth grader, I was a lowly sixth grader. Like Jennifer, a crowd of mostly boys always surrounded him, but he usually had a girl there, too. It was always one of the most popular girls with the right clothes, the right kind of body, and the right hair. Brad Morrow was our school's star. When he left middle school, a big hole opened no one could fill. Now he's the quarterback of the Mill Valley High School Vikings, and as a junior, he's even more crush-worthy. Of course,

Jennifer is his choice now. Although I'm convinced I have no chance with him, I still practice things to say if he ever looks my way.

"Oh, hi, I haven't seen you since middle school."

Nope, too lame. How dorky can I sound? No, it has to be just right. Not too eager and not too shy. Who am I kidding? I probably won't even get a word out if he looks at me. It'll be more like, "umph, umph, umph, uh, uh, uh."

He'll wonder if I can talk at all. I'd better wait and see what happens.

I'm lost in thought when the teacher decides to call on me. It's history, and since it's the beginning the year, it's all review so I'm lucky. I answer sounding as if I was paying attention all the time. Phew, it's a good thing my brain is on autopilot.

I glance at my watch after I finish answering the question.

"That's it for today, kids, but you have homework." I've already checked the board and written it, so I'm not listening.

As we file out of class, I'm feeling like I'm the wood in my father's vise on his worktable. At any minute, I could be squeezed so tight I might not be able to breathe.

The time has come for me to go to the mall with Jennifer. Becky and Janie meet me at our lockers, and we hurry to pile our books into our book bags.

"Janie and I were thinking about you all afternoon. Are you really going with her?"

"I told you guys at lunch."

Becky and Janie have this pleading don't go look in their eyes.

"I guess you have to go if it's important. I mean you need to have the stuff by tomorrow, right. So how did the idea for new jeans come up? I know how you feel about the new styles. Hope it isn't too horrible for you. Do you have enough money for new jeans? Have you told your mom?" Janie says without taking a breath.

Darn, Janie reminds me of the horror of the weekend before school when she and Becky went shopping with me. Maybe I won't get anything at all. But it would be nice to show up in new clothes, and maybe then if I run into Brad, he might notice me. I start making up these great meetings. "Earth to Carolyn, come in." Becky pokes me in the arm.

"Where were you? I asked did you call your mother." I must have tuned her out when I was dreaming about Brad.

"Sorry, I guess I have too much on my mind. No, because of this new project, she can't get calls before five o' clock. So I usually wait and call her then." I should be home before her, I think, and then I'll tell her all about it. "As long as I'm with Jennifer's mom, it will be okay," I say as we hurry down the hallway. "She won't mind at all if I went to the mall. What I will have to explain is the new outfit I might get. I'll have to pay for it from my own money, which means more babysitting. What a pain this survey is." We're almost to the front of the building.

I look at my watch and panic. It's two twenty-five, and I have to meet Jennifer soon, or I'll miss my ride. I race to the front of the school with Becky and Janie a few feet behind me. The full impact of what I'm about to do hits me. I could still catch the bus with my friends, and this would all be over. But if I run away now, Jennifer won't do the survey with me. She'll find some excuse to switch partners, and I'll have to be Mary's partner. Ugh! My throat feels like glue, and my legs feel rubbery.

Chapter Six

People throw Frisbees to each other on the grass in front of school, and buses line the curb. Parents wait in their cars with the air conditioning on, and kids with their own cars zoom past with music blaring. Over on the athletic field, some girls are getting ready to practice field hockey. Some kids run around the track on the football field. I feel calmer, and my muscles start to relax. As if on cue, the door opens, and Jennifer and her crowd spill out of school. She's talking to Maura, who looks very similar to Jennifer except with dark hair. Maura has an odd expression on her face and looks sick when she sees me.

"You're going with 'breathe, Carolyn, breathe'?" Maura feels Jennifer's forehead. "Just checking, but you're normal. What's going on here? Is this charity?"

"Maura, this is none of your business. But if you want to know so badly, it's for a school project. We have to go get materials. Do you think I would choose to be with her for fun?" Jennifer laughs loudly at this, tilting her head back.

Why did I come? I can still change my mind.

"Okay, give me a call when you get back," Maura says. "How are things going with Brad?"

"He's got practice again today. In fact, there he is now. I know if he's late, he'll be in a lot of trouble with his coach."

Brad Morrow, in his full practice football uniform complete with shoulder pads and short-sleeved purple jersey with Vikings in big letters and number 25 on the back, comes running over to Jennifer and her group. I wobble a little but manage to keep my balance and continue breathing. He looks so amazing. His dark, wavy hair, his chiseled features, and sky-blue eyes give me a funny feeling in my stomach. I realize how ridiculous I was to think he would ever speak to me. He grabs Jennifer around the waist and hugs her. Arm in arm, they start walking towards me.

"I'm going to the mall, and you can call me when I get back. Should be around fiveish. You have football practice today anyway."

Brad looks down at the ground and kicks a little dirt off his cleats." We haven't seen each other all week. I thought maybe after practice we'd hang out a little." Brad keeps looking down at his shoes like he's not too happy about this.

Jennifer throws a pouty look at Brad and says, "I want to spend time with you, too; you know that. We'll hang out tomorrow after school. I'll even watch your practice if you want me to."

Brad looks like it's his birthday or something. He has this ridiculous grin on his face.

"Sure that would bc great. I don't think the coach will mind. I've got to go now. I'll call you around five. Talk to you soon."

Brad starts running backward toward the field holding his helmet in one hand and waving to Jennifer with the other. I'm wondering how long he can run backward when I feel a hand on my shoulder.

"Carolyn, we'll wait here for my mom. She's usually on time, but maybe there's traffic or something."

As she's looking at Brad and waving too, he turns around and runs to get to the field.

Jennifer turns to me and says, "I actually thought you might not show up. I'm surprised you did. I thought your little dweeby friends might have talked you out of it."

"Jennifer, my life is my own. My friends don't dictate what I do. Do yours?"

"Spunky, aren't we?"

I am just as surprised as Jennifer at my answer. Where did that come from? I don't know where I got the courage to say something like that.

We spend the next few minutes in silence.

Jennifer's mom pulls up to the curb, which is now empty of buses, and we get into her expensive, leather seated SUV. It has a TV in back, and there are snacks and a tiny refrigerator. I'm afraid to eat anything, since I have to fit into the clothes.

Jennifer grabs a whole bag of chips. She asks me with her mouth full of chips, "Do you want any? "She opens the refrigerator and gets a can of soda.

"No, thank you, I'm fine," I say. Meanwhile she is gulping down the can of soda.

"You want some chocolates?" Jennifer holds out a box of expensive chocolates in a gold foil box.

With my mouth watering for the yummy taste, I resist and say, "No thank you." I have to sit on my hands to keep them from reaching for the box. How can she eat so much and look like she does? Must be a high metabolism I think, or lots of exercise. Does she dance or work out? This is a big surprise to me. Jennifer Taylor actually eats.

We arrive at the mall, and Jennifer's mom tells us to be in front at five. We agree and get out of the car. Entering the mall, I'm petrified. This is going to be the worst experience of my life. Jennifer excuses herself to go to the restroom, and I decide to sit and wait for her while she's in the restroom.

"Okay, Carolyn, let's get started. We have a couple of hours to do this. Let's not waste time," she says as she leaves the restroom and walks toward me.

It takes us no time at all to find the supplies we need for the project.

"Hey, we have a lot of time left, and since you need clothes, how about going around and seeing if you can get something better to wear?"

I break into a cold sweat. This is what I dreaded. Miss Perfect and me shopping for clothes together.

We walk toward one store that has those low-slung jeans in the window and mannequins for size zero.

"We'll start here and work our way toward the less fashionable places. Don't touch anything. I'll pick out the clothes for you. What size are you?"

I tell her I'm a size twelve. She looks at me like maybe I told her I committed a crime.

"You're a twelve? I don't know if they go that high here. Let me look, okay?"

I stand around feeling about four-years-old. Jennifer is picking out my clothes. Finally, she waves for me to come to the dressing rooms in the back, and she has a pile of clothes over both arms.

"Take something will you Carolyn? Oh, that's a relief. I thought my arms were going to break from all these clothes." She shakes out her arms as I grab one of the piles, and she lays the rest on the bench in front of us.

"Start trying on these things. We can't discard anything until we know what fits you and how it looks. Get going."

I get undressed, and I feel amazingly uncomfortable with Jennifer looking at me. It's okay to change in front of other girls you don't know in gym, but here it's just weird. I wish it were Becky and Janie here with me instead of Jennifer. I strip down to my underwear and pull on a pair of jeans, which barely make it over my thighs. Jennifer looks disgusted, but she says to try on the next pair. We go on like this for a full half hour, with me trying on everything in the pile. Finally, a pair of jeans seems to fit me and so does a top that goes with it. I model for Jennifer and think we're finished. Am I ever wrong!

"Carolyn, even though those fit you, just see how you look in them. You're bulging everywhere. No, you can't wear those. Take them off. We have to try another place."

Another place? I'm perspiring now, and I'm starving. Usually I have a snack after school, and it's an hour past the time I would have eaten.

"Jennifer, do we have to go anywhere else? I'm fine with these. I don't think they look bad."

"Get dressed, Carolyn. We're going to another store." Jennifer leaves the dressing room, and I finish getting dressed.

In the next store, Jennifer repeats what she did in the first one. I try on everything for her, and finally, we find one pair of jeans that fits me and are in style. I can't believe it. They are tight fitting, but they also don't show any bulges. Jennifer picks out a top to wear with them, which is way too tight for my usual taste. I look at myself in the mirror and barely recognize me. I almost look good, if I wasn't so big. The pants are eighty-five dollars. The top is forty-five dollars. I can't pay for these. I go to put them back, but Jennifer stops me.

"You have to buy those. They change you completely, and you won't embarrass me when we're doing our survey."

"But I don't have the money with me."

"Don't worry, I'll pay for this outfit. You'll owe me."

"You'll have to wait awhile 'till I get the money from babysitting."

"No problem. Let's go."

How will I pay for this with my babysitting money? Oh well, I have awhile to do that. Meanwhile, Jennifer pays with her credit card, and we leave the store. My stomach is growling, and I can't go on anymore.

"Couldn't we get a little something to eat?" I plop myself down in the Food Court and refuse to budge.

"Yeah, I could go for a little something. How about a pretzel? Or maybe a frozen yogurt? What do you want, Carolyn? I'm buying."

I decide to have both. I'm hungry, and I did all that work trying on clothes. So, we go to both places and get a pretzel and a cone of frozen yogurt for each of us. We find a table and lick our cones and stuff pieces of the soft pretzel into our mouths. I'm almost feeling relaxed now. This is not the Jennifer I know in school. We've been together for almost two hours, and she hasn't been as mean to me. I'm beginning to feel we might be friends, at least outside of school.

"Carolyn, when we get to school tomorrow, you will forget any of this happened, right?"

So much for us being friends.

"Sure Jennifer, we'll go our usual ways. I won't talk to you, and you won't talk to me, except when we have to, okay?"

"Yes, that will be perfect."

She finishes her cone and pretzel quickly, and we go to the restroom. This time I have to go, but Jennifer dawdles outside the stalls doing her makeup until I come out. I finish up and tell her I'll meet her outside. Again, I have to wait for her for a long time. While I'm waiting, I have time to think. How will I explain the clothes I just bought? My mother would never let me buy a pair of pants for that price. I'll have to say they were on sale, and they didn't change the price on the ticket. She might buy it. Jennifer comes out of the restroom, and we walk toward the front entrance. The SUV pulls up after we've been waiting about fifteen minutes in complete silence.

"Carolyn, I'll take you home. Your mom will be worrying about you, since you didn't call her," Mrs. Taylor says.

"Oh, she doesn't worry about me. She gets home around ten usually. I get my own dinner, since my dad is usually late, too."

"I didn't know that. How awful for you. Well, in that case, you can have dinner with us. We have plenty of food, and it will be fun for Jennifer to have one of her friends to dinner. Won't it Jen?"

Jennifer gives her mother a tight smile without using her eyes.

"I don't know if I can accept your invitation, Mrs. Taylor. I have a lot of work to do, and I'm sure Jennifer does, too."

"Oh, she can get it done after dinner. I'll take you home right afterward, so you can get your homework done, or you can start some of it at our house. Right, Jen?"

Jennifer looks like she's going to be sick.

I decide it can't be so bad, and besides, I'll get to know Jennifer a little better. That was my plan, right?

"Well, if it won't be too much trouble. I'll come over. But I have to go home immediately after dinner, so my dad won't worry about me. He's usually home by seven-thirty. Do you think we'll be finished by then? Or should I call him now?"

I decide to call my dad as soon as we get to Jennifer's house. Mrs. Taylor pulls up to their house, a large white one with lots of windows and columns in front. The driveway curves and circles a grassy area in the middle. Mrs. Taylor carries in the groceries. I follow her and Jennifer through the door.

Chapter Seven

The inside of Jennifer's house looks like a page out of *Architectural Digest*. I used to leaf through those at my grandmother's house when I was a little girl and imagine I lived in one of the houses on those pages. Now I'm walking on the parquet floors of one of them. We walk through the house into the kitchen at the back, and Mrs. Taylor tells me to go with Jennifer to drop off my book bag and leave my packages in her room. I follow Jennifer up the stairs to her room on the second floor. Jennifer's room is amazing. I plop my book bag down on her pink rug and stare at her room as if I were in Disney World. She has a four-poster bed with ruffled curtains around the sides draped over from the top, and a pink comforter with tiny rosebuds covers the bed. Pillows of every size spill over the comforter. One very bedraggled rag doll is in the center of the largest pillow. I wonder why such a messy looking doll is being displayed.

I take out my cell phone and dial Dad's number. I get his answering machine and leave a short message so he won't be nervous about where I am.

The phone rings, and Jennifer answers it.

"Brad, we just got back from the mall. What an experience. Remind me never to go shopping after school again."

Jennifer listens to Brad on the other end.

"Of course, I wish we could have been together. Yes, you have to be patient. Saturday will come soon. Where do you want to go? Oh, listen, can you hang on for a second someone's calling me." Jennifer hits her flash button. "Hi Maura, yes we went to the mall. No I'll call you back later. Can't talk, Brad was on the line when you called. What was it like? Can't talk now; call me back on my cell, okay?"

I guess Maura got off the line, because Jennifer keeps talking to Brad.

"Sorry to keep you waiting Brad; Maura called. No, that's okay. I'll call her back later. I'd rather talk to you. Ha, ha, ha, no it wasn't so bad…"

The conversation continues until Mrs. Taylor calls us to dinner. I hang around and try not to ogle all of Jennifer's things. I have nothing to do, so I've been trying the doors. She has two closets full of clothes. One of them is so big you could call it a room. I find the bathroom on the other side of her room by accident. She has her own whirlpool bath and a glass-door shower. I love this room. Too bad she isn't a real friend. Jennifer finishes her phone conversation, and we go downstairs.

Mrs. Taylor has made a quick dinner of hog dogs and baked potatoes with a salad and hot dog rolls. I'm starving, even though we just had a snack. Jennifer eats three hot dogs like me, so I don't feel so bad about pigging out. Mrs. Taylor hardly eats. She is as thin as Jennifer. We have store-bought chocolate cake for dessert. Jennifer excuses herself and goes upstairs. I follow her to get my book bag. She isn't in her room, but I hear sounds as I stand outside her bathroom door. They sound like retching, and I wonder if Jennifer is sick. I decide to wait and see if she's all right. I sit on her bed. Finally, Jennifer comes out and glares at me.

"Carolyn, what are you doing up here?"

I tell her the truth. "I had to get my things before I go home. Are you feeling okay?"

"Sure, why? Oh, you heard me in the bathroom? I guess the hot dogs didn't agree with me. I have this condition. It's nothing. I'm used to it."

"Oh, if you're okay, that's fine with me. I guess that's how you stay so thin all the time. I mean we ate the same amount of stuff. You don't gain an ounce, and I keep getting fatter. It's a curse I have.

I can't resist food, and the weight piles on me. I wish I could lose weight."

I know I'm talking too much, but something doesn't feel right here, and I always talk too much when I'm nervous. I guess I'm just a mess with the breathing thing and the talking too much. I'm wondering why Jennifer would even bother with me; I suppose she had no choice with her mom inviting me. She's just being polite for her sake.

"Carolyn, are you almost ready to go? You wanted to leave right after dinner," Mrs. Taylor calls up the stairs.

"Yes, I'm coming." I bound downstairs, eager to leave Jennifer's house.

I have a feeling Jennifer is lying. But why would she lie? Was perfect Jennifer not so perfect after all? Suddenly I feel a whole lot better.

I thank Mrs. Taylor for the dinner and the rides, and I'm smiling as I leave the SUV and walk to my door. Dad opens the door and hugs me. Max is there with his tail wagging, and I lean down and hug him around the neck, his familiar, sweet, Newfoundland smell telling me I'm home. I look around at my own house that is not out of the pages of *Architectural Digest*. The brick red paint is peeling, and the gutters are sagging, but I love it here. I walk upstairs to my own room and dump my book bag on the floor. It's an old beige carpet, but what the hell. It's mine, and it's comfortable. My room. Pictures of my favorite movie, TV, and music stars are pasted all over my wall like wallpaper. Every time I find one I like, I clip it out and put it on my wall. Tonight I'll do my homework and lay my new clothes on the chair for tomorrow. How wonderful to wake up to these clothes for a change.

I open the bag with the clothes and take out the jeans and top. I take off all the tags and arrange the new jeans and top on the chair near my bed. It's like the chair has been revived. My whole room looks better. I can't wait for tomorrow. I start my homework and feel a tremendous weight lift from my shoulders. I'll have the right jeans on in the morning. What does it matter if I'll have to baby-sit for the rest of my life to pay for them?

* * * *

The next morning, I race downstairs in my new outfit. Mom hasn't seen it yet, so I'm anxious for her reaction when she sees me. I don't have long to wait. She looks up while she's raising her coffee mug to her lips. Startled she almost drops it.

"What are you wearing, Carolyn? Where did you get that outfit? I hope you have an explanation for this!" She gives me that mother vision look.

Stay calm, I say to myself. Breathe and stay calm. She'll be okay with this soon.

"I went with Jennifer Taylor to the mall yesterday and bought this. Don't you love it on me?"

"Jennifer Taylor, Jonathan Taylor's daughter? Are you two friends now? Didn't you say she bothered you all last year? What happened?" She continues to peer into my eyes.

This is much harder than I thought it would be.

"Well, I saw how everyone was dressed in school the other day, and I decided I had to have some decent clothes. I couldn't call you, because of the after five o'clock rule, so I went and got these. I had dinner over at Jennifer's house last night. Didn't Dad tell you when you got home?"

"No, Dad was asleep when I got home, and it was so late I didn't want to wake you. Okay, how much were they?"

I couldn't get a break, could I?

"I got them on sale, and they were half price. I had some babysitting money saved I used, so don't worry."

I'd have to ask around so I could babysit to make the money to pay Jennifer. Meanwhile, Mom didn't need to know everything.

47

"I love the way they fit you. I wonder why we didn't see these when we went on Saturday." Her expression has definitely softened.

"We went to a different store. Jennifer is great about clothes. She helped me find this outfit. Her house is really neat, too. She has a huge room and her own bathroom with a whirlpool bathtub. How cool is that?"

Making Mom feel guilty might take her attention away from the prices.

"If your Dad owned half this town, we'd have a house like that, too. Get ready, we have to go." She smiles at me, and I let out my breath.

On the ride to school, I wonder how Jennifer will treat me. At least I have on the right clothes now.

"Carolyn, wait up," Becky says when I get to school and runs to catch up with me in the hall.

"Where were you around seven o'clock yesterday? I called and got your answering machine. I also called your cell but got voice mail. So then I wondered if you had gotten back from the mall yet."

"Well, I met my dad downtown, since Mom wasn't coming home until late, and we had dinner together." I look Becky straight in the eyes as I say this and pray she'll believe me. "Oh, yeah, my phone needed to be recharged."

Whew, was I going to have to lie all day? I feel my breakfast repeating in my throat. I should be feeling terrific, but instead I have this bitter acid taste in my mouth. First Mom and now Becky. I never lied to Becky before yesterday, and now I wonder why I haven't told her the truth. This is getting more and more complicated.

Becky takes a good look at me. Her eyes get wider, and she stares in disbelief.

"Carolyn, what are you wearing? Oh, my God, you found a pair of those pants in your size. Where did you find them? Wow, they fit you great. And I love the top, too. The whole outfit makes you look so thin."

Becky, you're such a good friend. What am I doing to you? Yet another part of me is cheering me on to keep my dinner with Jennifer a secret.

The bell rings for first period, and kids scatter everywhere. Becky and I move toward my math classroom and say goodbye at the door. When it's time for us to work on our projects, Mr. Armbruster asks if anyone has started their survey. Luckily, not one person has, and I'm happy to hear this. He tells us we have only two days to complete it, and we have to begin by lunchtime today. We have a half hour to meet with our partners.

Jennifer has moved the desks together and waits for me at her desk. We don't actually greet each other, but I can tell something has changed in the way she speaks to me.

"Carolyn, you look so much better today. Didn't I tell you we'd find something you could wear? Now let's decide how we're going to do this survey. We'll have to start at lunch and interview all the people we know first. I brought the clipboard so we'll have something to write on. How many people do you know? I know at least fifty, so we might not even have to interview anyone else."

"That's great, Jennifer. By the way, dinner was great last night. Please thank your mother for me. I also appreciate your paying for this outfit. I'll pay you back as soon as I get the money from babysitting."

"It was worth it to make you into a human being. I feel like Professor Dolittle in *My Fair Lady*. It's amazing what clothes can do for a person."

I'm feeling better than ever about myself when she says, "Now if you were only a little bit thinner. You should concentrate on what you eat."

So much for feeling good about myself—Jennifer's comments make me feel like garbage. I'll never have the right look, and who am

I kidding? Is this worth lying to my best friend? I decide to tell Becky and Janie after all. But then I will have to explain why I lied this morning. No, maybe it was better to keep everything I did with Jennifer a secret. I don't like this division in myself.

At lunchtime, I have to rush my yogurt, and I race over to Jennifer's table to the astonishment of my friends. I don't even have time to explain to Becky and Janie. I feel bad, but I have to do this project, and we have so little time. Jennifer barely glances at me, but she gets up and hands me the clipboard.

"Okay, go and get your few friends to give you their choices, and then we'll do mine."

Walking back to my table, I wonder if Becky and Janie will even speak to me at all. I've been a real pain lately, and they have every right to ignore me.

"Carolyn, what are you doing racing all over the lunchroom? Are you on speed?"

"No, guys, actually I'm in the middle of this survey we have to do for math. Sorry I ran away like that, but I had to get the clipboard from Jennifer. Could you please help me out with this? I have to know what your favorite foods are. We have to get the favorite foods of at least fifty people in school and make a graph of the choices. I pretty much know your favorite foods, but they might have changed over the summer."

Becky answers first. "I love French fries. Give me a plate of French fries, and I'm in heaven."

Janie thinks for a minute. "Chocolate ice cream, yup give me a bowl or a cone of chocolate ice cream, and I'm happy."

Becky and Janie's favorite foods are exactly the same as always. Nothing about either of them seems to have changed. I feel like I'm on the outside of a walled city, and suddenly I've lost the key to my own world. I feel tears start at the corners of my eyes. I wipe them away.

I write down their choices on the list and look around for someone else I know. This is pathetic, because I don't know anyone else well enough to go over and ask their favorite food. So I stroll back to Jennifer's table and hand her the clipboard.

"Okay, we have two people, only forty-eight more to go. It's your turn now, I guess."

"Do you really only know two people here? Your life is worse than I thought. I'll start here at this table."

Jennifer turns to the person on her right.

"We're doing this food thing for math, and we have to ask people what their favorite foods are. Can you tell me what your favorite food is?"

Maura answers, "Jen you know what my favorite food is, we've been friends since the first grade."

"I know, but we're supposed to ask. It might have changed, you know."

"All right, my favorite food, as you know, is chunky peanut butter. I love to take fingerfuls from the jar and lick my fingers. Yummy."

"Nope, you haven't changed since first grade. I remember those afternoons when we used to sneak the peanut butter jar out of the pantry and eat the peanut butter with our fingers. You still do that now? It's so fattening. I haven't had peanut butter in ages."

A faraway expression appears in Jennifer's eyes like she's remembering a great feeling she'll never have again.

Jennifer writes down the answer in the proper column and then turns to the person on her left, who has his back turned to me. He turns quickly when he hears her voice.

"Brad, do you think you could help me with this food survey thing?"

It's Brad Morrow, a foot in front of me. I'm glad I have on my brand new outfit. Maybe Jennifer will introduce us. I wait, realizing I've become invisible again. Did I think Jennifer would bring me into her circle of friends? I'm just doing a school project with her, and she felt sorry for me and bought me an outfit, for which I have to pay her back, soon. I'm standing so close to Brad I can reach out and touch his shoulder, so my body starts doing weird things. My palms are clasped together in front of me and begin to sweat. I get this loopy thing in my stomach, and I worry I might have one of my non-breathing attacks. I force myself to keep breathing as I stand in front of the one boy who can make me turn to mush. Jennifer doesn't seem to be having any trouble talking with him, and he gives her his choice, finally. I couldn't have stood here another moment without fainting.

"I love pizza, especially with pepperoni."

I gasp, and without thinking, I burst out, "Oh, wow, I love it too; that's my favorite food."

Jennifer and Brad turn around to look at me. Jennifer's eyes bore into mine, telling me I goofed.

I glance at Brad not wanting to see Jennifer's eyes. His are warm and welcoming. An expression of surprise is on his face.

Brad says to me, "Who are you? Did we meet?"

The words seem harsh and might have made me run away if I hadn't seen the expression in his eyes. I guess he is just curious. So I stay where I am.

"Brad, this is Carolyn. Carolyn, this is Brad. She's doing this survey thing with me. Now you're introduced.'"

"Pleased to meet you. So you like pizza with pepperoni, too. Don't have the cafeteria pizza. It sucks, but I eat it 'cause I'm starved." Brad gives me a big smile.

"Hi." I smile back and feel special.

I can't believe I can squeak even that out. My tongue almost sticks to the roof of my mouth it's so dry. Jennifer actually introduced me. All I could say was hi. You can't go wrong with a simple word like that, though.

Before Jennifer can ask anyone else about their favorite food, the bell rings, and we have to leave. The whole table gets up, and without saying goodbye to me, Jennifer leaves, too. Well, I'm not totally invisible all the time. I do materialize for a few minutes, like a ghost. Ha, ha, I'm a ghost haunting Jennifer now. Whoo, how scary? Get a grip on yourself Carolyn. I think this whole business is making you nutty. Darn right, I've gone from being invisible to being a ghost. What next?

Sitting at home after a fairly normal afternoon at school, munching on chocolate sandwich cookies and milk, I ponder the whole Jennifer business. She appears perfect on the outside, and she has loads of friends. She has the greatest boyfriend ever, Brad, whose name I can barely think without getting all goose bumpy. Her clothes are absolutely gorgeous and always in style. Yet I think she is unhappy. Something isn't right. Why does she go to the restroom so much? Was she really sick last night? Why eat if you can't keep it in you. I love food, so I don't understand how anyone can do this. Or is her mom fooling herself into thinking Jennifer really has a bladder problem because she drinks too much? She told me last night in the car on the way home. We had this tight conversation.

"Mrs. Taylor," I asked her, "does Jennifer have a problem that makes her go to the bathroom a lot?"

She kept her eyes on the road, but she said, "Well, actually, she does have a little bladder problem."

Bladder problem? I didn't think so. That doesn't make you throw up most of the time.

I want to help Jennifer to stop doing that thing she does. I think she is bulimic. We learned about it in health class last year. Yuck. Shouldn't her mom be giving her some kind of help if she knows? I didn't know how, but maybe we could both help each other. She could help me become a cheerleader, and then I'd be popular. Maybe I could help her stop what she's doing to herself.

I hadn't realized it until today, but I am desperate to be popular. If I were popular, I could be closer to Brad. Actually what I want is to get Brad to notice me. Now I am just one more of Jennifer's groupies to him. I want him to see me as myself and to want to be with me. It's a stupid dream, but I can't get rid of it. Now I've met him and seen him up close, I know that dream will never leave me until it happens. All I have to figure out is how to make it happen.

Chapter Eight

It's Thursday, the last day for getting our survey done. Before I leave the house, I get a phone call.

"Carolyn, pick up the phone. It's Jennifer."

Jennifer is calling me before school? What could she want?

"Hi, Jennifer," I say. "Can I do something for you?"

"Yes, actually, we have to finish this stupid survey today, and I only did a few more people yesterday. I'll meet you out front, and we'll do it then. Remember to dress as cool as you did yesterday. I have a reputation to uphold. Be there about fifteen minutes early, so we can get everyone we have to survey."

"Okay, Jennifer, I'll try. I'm sure my mom won't mind taking me a little earlier. See you at eight. Bye."

I hang up the phone and look in my closet for a decent top. Finally, I pick out the only top that isn't a sweatshirt. It's blue and tighter than my other shirts, but it's last year's, and I hope it will do. I fly downstairs and tell Mom we have to leave right now. One thing about Mom is she doesn't mind going anywhere early. She likes to take her time before work and get into the office before everyone else. So we race out of the house, and I make it to school exactly by eight.

This time Jennifer is waiting for me by the curb, and as I get to where she's standing, she tells me, "I brought two clipboards, so we can get everyone who is walking into the school. You take the right door, and I'll take the left door. We should hit on everyone that way."

"But, Jennifer, these are your friends. Will they talk to me?"

"I'll tell them we're doing this together, and they have to talk to you. The top is a little out of style, but it will have to do. You should have bought two shirts the other day. Remember to go back and buy a second one so you can switch off."

"Thanks, Jennifer, I'll try this weekend." How can she keep doing that? Why did I agree? I don't even know myself anymore. This has to end. Only one more day. Thank goodness!

Jennifer hands me a clipboard. She has copied the survey list, so we each have a copy. We take our places opposite each other by the front doors.

People get off the arriving buses. I stop the first person I see and ask him about his favorite food. Jennifer sees him, and he says hi to her. They're friends, and Jennifer tells him to give me the answer. I get his choice, and it goes like that for whoever walks by me. Jennifer is right. She does know fifty people. When the first bell rings, we have over forty people altogether. All we need is eight more people. We can get those easily at lunchtime. Jennifer almost smiles at me.

"Good job, Carolyn. You're better at this than I thought you'd be. Maybe you can be made into a real person after all."

Was this supposed to be a compliment? I guess it was the best she could do.

We hurry to our lockers where I find Becky and Janie have gone to class already. We can't have our usual morning talk. Oh well, at least I'll see Becky today at lunch and gym. I'll explain everything to her then.

I rush to math class and make it just as the last bell rings. Catching my breath, I try to pay attention to the homework Mr. Armbruster is giving us. I'm happy we're going to be able to get our survey done on time. I hear a lot of kids telling each other they didn't get enough people yet. If we get eight more people at lunch, Jennifer and I will be able to make our graph tomorrow in class.

Mr. Armbruster tells us today we are going to make a practice graph with the data we have collected so far. Tomorrow we will add the rest of the data to our final graphs. So we have to work on our graphs with our partners. He hands out graph paper and tells us to get started. We have been given the rubric, so I take it out and see what we have to do. We have our choice of any type of graph to show our results. First we have to tally each food and find out how many of each food people chose. Jennifer decides I should do this, so I make a list of the foods and tally them. I add up the numbers and write each number next to the appropriate food. It looks like the favorite food so far is French fries, with pizza a close second, followed by ice cream. We won't know for sure until we get the last eight. We decide to do a bar graph, the easiest kind. Jennifer is so much better at art than I am, so she does the basic graph. She labels it, and it's amazing how neat it is. She's perfect at making graphs, too. She draws the lines for each food, and we both color them in. I've got markers, so we use mine. Our graph is finished before everyone else's, and so we have nothing left to do.

"Jennifer, I have a problem maybe you can help me?"

"Fine, what's your problem? I've got nothing to do for a few minutes. Maybe I can help you."

"I have this crush on a boy in school, and I can't get him to notice me. What can I do?"

"Who is he? Do I know him?"

"I'm not sure." Now this is tricky, because I haven't figured out who I should say I have a crush on. I'll have to make up someone she doesn't know."

"He's a junior, but I don't think you know him. He might be new because I don't remember him from middle school at all."

I don't give him a name. It wouldn't do to have a crush on someone who isn't worthy of one. I'll have to check the yearbook and find someone. Meanwhile, I didn't need to have Jennifer know who it is yet.

"I don't know his name. I only know when I see him I melt. What can I do?"

"First thing you need to do is lose weight. Do you do any exercise, dance, run, play tennis?" I want to cry, but I'll bet Jennifer doesn't realize she's hurt me, and I can't let her see any tears. I think of Brad, and my tears vanish.

"No, I wanted to try out for cheerleading, but I had to have the physical during the summer, and I missed the deadline. Anyway you've seen how I tumble. I'd never make the team."

Jennifer gives me a blank stare. "You are one of the most pathetic people I've ever met. Can't you do anything? You could always walk."

"Do you think you could help me with my somersaults and tumbling?"

"That depends on whether you have any potential at all. I can't be wasting my time on a no talent wannabe." Jennifer's eyes bore into me like a power drill.

"I think if I could get a few pointers, I'll improve. I really want to be a cheerleader, and I know you are amazing in gymnastics."

Jennifer nods her head.

"I guess your gymnastics is the way you stay so thin."

"It's not easy for me to stay thin. I like to eat, too, but I have to stay a certain weight for gymnastics. It's tough, but I do it. "

"Do you think losing weight will help me become a cheerleader and get my crush to notice me?"

Yes, Carolyn,

"If you've noticed, you don't have a bad-looking face. If you lost a little weight, you could be great looking, and if you did something different with your hair, that might help, too." Jennifer's eyes light up, and I start to worry. What does she have in store for me now?

"I'll tell you what. Why don't you let me help you change? I've spent a few days with you, and you're not so bad. I guess you can't help your breathing problem, but aside from that, I've actually enjoyed myself with you."

Okay, she is actually saying nice things about me.

"You're not a big talker, and you do what you're told. We'll make you into someone nobody will be able to resist."

I'm starting to get excited myself.

"Also, when I can, I'll work with you on your tumbling. Of course, you'll have to work a little. I can only do so much you know." Jennifer stops talking finally.

I think this is probably the most she has ever said to me at one time.

Yes, this is wonderful. Jennifer is going to help me to change myself. I'm one step closer to my goal. She is much nicer than I thought. I vow to help her, too. She'll help me learn to tumble and become popular, and I'll find something I can do for her. If it means getting closer to Brad, I'll try it. Also, maybe I'll get up enough nerve to try out for cheerleading next time.

I float in a happy haze out of the door and through my morning classes. Not until lunchtime do I come back to earth. Darn, what will Becky and Janie think when I start hanging out with Jennifer; that is if she will talk to me in school? Maybe this will all have to be done in secret. In the meantime, no one has to know about our decision.

Becky is waiting for me at our usual table. They ran out of yogurt today, so I'm settling for salad with no dressing. I set down my tray, and Becky starts talking.

"Carolyn, where were you this morning? I didn't see you in front of school at our usual place. I looked for you at the lockers, and you weren't there. Were you late?"

"No. I was doing that survey thing with Jennifer. We were by the front doors, but you must have missed us. We got over forty people, twenty apiece."

"Oh, that's great Carolyn. What is she like, I mean, you know as a person?"

"I was kind of frightened of her at first, but she's turning out to be okay. She tolerates me I guess. I feel kind of invisible when I'm with her. She knows all these people, and when we aren't doing the survey, she doesn't even talk to me. It's kind of spooky. One minute we're talking, and the next minute she's totally ignoring me."

"What did you expect? At least she isn't bothering you with that ridiculous 'breathe, Carolyn, breathe' routine. I was so sick of it last year."

"Yes, well maybe she's grown up a little bit. I can actually stand her a little."

"I guess she wouldn't be so bad if she wasn't so incredibly perfect in every way."

"That does get to me, but I'm sure there is something at which she is not perfect."

"If there is, she hides it very well. Anyway, we have gym today, don't we?"

"Yes, and I hope everyone's forgotten about Monday by now. I felt so stupid about that ridiculous fainting. I wish I had it totally under control now, but I never know when I will get into a panic again."

"Oh, Carolyn, you're fine. You just need to remember to breathe. I can remind you, but it might bring back memories from last year. Take a deep breath and let it out slowly, so your breathing will go back to normal. Anyway, you know Jennifer now, and nothing else should bother you. Let's get going, so we get to gym on time."

We finish our food and head to the gym. We're early, but the bell is about to ring to end the period. The locker room doors open, and the girls who had gym last period come flooding out. I'm about to walk into the locker room when I see Jennifer duck into the Girls' room. Why does she go to the bathroom so much? Becky and I see Janie come out of the locker room, and we wave and smile at each other. We hardly see each other anymore. I miss middle school a lot. Yet, I feel high school is going to change all of us so much we won't be able to find our middle school selves anymore. I'm already different from the beginning of the year. In the next few weeks, I might alter myself even more. Am I ready for such change? I don't think so, because I know it is going to take me further away from my old friends. Suddenly I am afraid of what is to come. But I have taken the first step on the road to becoming popular.

This time in gym, I'm completely different. Becky turns around in line and gives me a big smile. I mentally hit myself over the head. I'm such a jerk to do this to Becky, but I can't seem to stop myself. The image of Brad smiling is in my brain, and that keeps me going. I have to become popular and have Brad really notice me. I turn around to Jennifer, and she gives me a half smile.

Miss Gaylon finishes her attendance and comes over to me immediately.

"Miss Samuels I expected to see you back in class on Monday. However, I realize the episode with the food poisoning made getting back to class almost impossible. So I am excusing you from getting the note."

Phew, that was over.

We play indoor volleyball today, and I'm on a team opposite Becky and Jennifer. When the ball comes to me, I jump up and get it over the net. I continue to be able to play well. Something has happened to me. I can play volleyball. Maybe I got taller. Who cares? My team wins the game, and we get to shower first. Everyone from the team congratulates me on my great plays at the net. Maybe volleyball is my sport. I think about trying out for the volleyball team next fall. I know of a couple of girls who got NCAA scholarships for volleyball.

Back in the locker room after my shower, I get dressed quickly so I'll make the bus. Jennifer passes me.

"Carolyn, you surprise me. I never saw you play so well. I'll definitely help you." She walks out of the locker room with Maura and her usual crowd, and I feel like I'm living in a dream.

"I'm running to the bus, Becky, are you ready?"

"Just a second, I'll be done in a minute. You had a head start. Where did you learn to play so well? I've never seen you play like that?" Becky says pulling off her shirt and shorts. "It was like seeing a different person out there. I couldn't believe it." Becky slaps my hand and finishes dressing. "You got all of those balls over the net. Amazing."

We hurry to the bus, but we get separated. I look for her, and I'm not watching where I'm going. I have to catch this bus or wait another half hour. I have too much homework to waste my time waiting for the late bus. I see our bus ahead of me, and Becky running toward it. I try to catch up with her, and I walk without looking ahead of me. *Plunk,* I slam into the book bag of the person in front of me and practically fall on top of him. Our legs lock, and we fall down together in a heap. People are running for the bus and don't stop to help us. So I lie on the book bag attached to the person who peeks his head around to see who is on top of him.

"Aren't you Carolyn from lunch?" Brad says.

I bumped into Brad Morrow. Wasn't life ridiculous? And he remembered me.

"Are you okay?" he says.

I get to my feet and check if anything is hurt. Aside from a little dirt from the ground, which I brush off, I'm not hurt except for my knee, which I ignore. "I fell on top of you, so your book bag cushioned me."

Brad gets up, and I see he's got a little dirt on his knee. "Are you hurt? You seem to be able to walk, and that's good."

"Yes, I'm fine. Are you okay? I'm sorry for bumping into you. I was running to get my bus, and I didn't see you."

How did I have the courage to say all this? Must be shock, that's why I can talk with him.

"I understand. These things happen to me all the time on the football field. Better hurry. Is that your bus pulling away now?"

Wow, he's really nice, too. My cheeks get warm, and I realize I'm blushing. How embarrassing.

I see my bus starting to leave, and I rush toward it, waving frantically. Luckily, Becky sees me and tells the bus driver to stop. The driver pulls over and opens the doors.

"You could be killed doing something stupid like that. Don't ever do that again, or I'll have to report you," the bus driver says.

"I'm sorry. I fell on the way, and I was late. I was afraid the bus would leave without me." The driver doesn't look like she cares. "I promise it won't happen again."

She motions for me to get seated, and we leave the school. Another day has ended, and I think one more day, Friday. TGIF, only four days have passed, and I feel like a year has gone by there has been so much packed into this week.

Sitting by Becky, I wonder if she will speak to me again after what I am about to do. Shouldn't I tell her I am about to change myself completely? Or should I let her see me as a new person after the weekend? I'm so quiet on the bus ride home. Becky must think it's because I'm still getting over my accident. My knee starts throbbing, and I realize I've probably hurt it. But who can think of pain? I'm thinking about Brad and how he smiled at me. I can't wait to call Jennifer and plan my makeover tonight.

Chapter Nine

It's Friday. It's Friday...my alarm says with a loud, insistent beep. I spring out of bed anxious for the day to begin. Mr. Armbruster decided to have us stop doing our survey and do something else. Now we're going to finish it today. Okay, it's taken Jennifer three weeks to find a free Friday night, but it's really happening now. I'll either be jumping for joy tonight or ready to cut my throat. It's Operation Makeover tonight at Jennifer's house. I packed my bag last night, since I'm going straight from school. I think about how Mom took this while I'm getting dressed.

When Mom heard I was spending the night at Jennifer's house, she treated me like a cashmere sweater.

"Of course, Carolyn, you can spend the night there. I'll call Veronica to let her know it's okay. We know each other from the PTA. You're going to have so much fun."

Mom went on about how she remembered slumber parties from high school, but I tuned her out at this point. I noticed her expression, though, like I'd been crowned Miss Prom Queen or something. I wonder how she'll feel when she sees the new me tomorrow.

I start having trouble with my breathing when I think about the change in me. What will my hair look like? Will I like it? I'm starting to feel lightheaded and realize I'm holding my breath. Pull yourself together Carolyn and breathe. I should probably start timing myself to see how long I can go without breathing, but most times I don't even know I'm doing it. Like now; so it's a shock to feel the cool air rushing into my lungs finally.

I decide to splash some water on my face and brush my teeth. I tell myself to hold together and pad into the bathroom to get ready for school. On the way, I catch a glimpse of me in the mirror. Was I the same jerk who wouldn't go to school on that first Monday because I didn't like my clothes? Was I wrong or did my jeans fit better? I touch the fastening button, and I can put a finger into the waistband. I think I've lost weight, or maybe the jeans stretched. No. Must have lost weight. Wow, and in only three weeks.

Gathering my book bag and suitcase, I run downstairs, eager to get to school. I place them in front of the door and come back to the kitchen where Mom is drinking her usual before-driving-coffee.

I'm not even hungry, but I grab a slice of whole wheat bread and some orange juice.

"Carolyn, is that all you're going to eat?"

"Yeah, I'm not hungry. Anyway, I'll have a big lunch. We always send out for food on Fridays."

That's true. We got into this habit last year in middle school and decided to continue this year. Becky, Janie, and I get take out Chinese food delivered. I love to have Chow Fun. Yum, thinking about those delicious soft wide noodles and the meat, shrimp, and chicken pieces makes my mouth water. Can't wait. But first, Jennifer and I have to do our final graph of the food survey.

Before I know it I'm in math class.

"Ladies and gentlemen," Mr. Armbruster addresses our class. "Today is the last day for your food surveys. I know we put this aside for a while, so get out your folders. Now everyone, no matter how many people have been interviewed, will make a graph and finish your project today. Are there any questions? Just for fun, how many people were able to get fifty or more people for your survey?"

Jennifer and I raise our hands. No one joins us. Mr. Armbruster has this look of dull surprise on his face.

"Miss Samuels and Miss Taylor, who would have believed this? Congratulations, girls. You will have an A to start off your project. Good teamwork, and for the rest of you, do the best you can and help each other. Today we'll be going to the computer room to do our graphs. You have one half hour before we go to total and plot your graphs."

Jennifer and I have already done a practice graph, but we have to add on the extra people we interviewed. We divide up the work, and I wind up totaling the French fry people. French fries are most people's favorite food. Next comes pizza and third is ice cream. The fourth choice is candy. We decide to make little pictures of French fries, pizza, and ice cream for our cover. I start to draw the pictures and lose track of time until Mr. Armbruster reminds us it's time to go to the computer lab to make our graphs using Excel.

In the computer lab, Jennifer and I work together at one screen. I type because I'm so much faster. It's fun doing something better than Jennifer. First we add the data; then we make the graph. It's simple, and with our great head start, we finish first. Kids are standing around the printer waiting for their graphs. Ours comes out looking perfect. We rush over to Mr. Armbruster and hand it to him. The pictures on the cover look great, and I'm really proud of our work. We're free for the rest of the period, so Jennifer and I start talking. It's the kind of talking Becky, Janie, and I do, so I feel a little peculiar.

"Carolyn, how's it going with that guy you were telling me about a couple of days ago?"

"You know it's kind of funny, but the other day we sort of bumped into each other."

"What do you mean? Like you met at the mall or in town?"

"No, I mean we got all tangled up and fell. It was bizarre, really. I was late for my bus and wasn't watching where I was going. I even scraped my knee. See."

I pull up my jeans and show her the mark on my knee which is practically gone by now.

"Well, what did he say to you? Is he worth it? You know looks aren't everything."

I'm feeling both hot and cold at the same time, like standing under a shower that's constantly changing temperatures. Can my deodorant stand this pressure? I'll say Brad's name any minute, and then where will I be? I'm supposed to be made over tonight. I don't want to spoil that. I can hold it in.

I'm pretty confident when out of the corner of my eye I see Brad sauntering towards the computer room. I pretend I need to get something from my bag and duck down. Too late I see a pair of feet in front of me.

"What are you guys doing here?"

"Brad, do you have a free period now? How come you're here?" Jennifer looks up with surprise.

"My history teacher wants me to do this dumb presentation on PowerPoint, and he gave me the time to do it now. All of the computers in the room were taken. So, here I am. "

"We had to do a graph. Carolyn and I got an A for part of it, because we interviewed fifty people for our survey. But we just clinched it with an amazing graph."

While they are talking, I'm doing my breathing thing. By the time they are finished, I'm practically fainting. Jennifer looks over at me. I'm trying to hide by looking for something in my bag, but I pick up my face for a minute.

"Carolyn, what the hell? Are you having that problem again?"

I'm sure I must be turning purple, but I can't seem to breathe. This time I refuse to faint. I will myself to take a breath. One, two, three…

"Whew." I open my mouth and take in the stale air of the computer room.

"Wow, I thought you'd be down on the floor again. You are scary. I almost had to say, breathe, Carolyn, breathe. Ha, ha, ha, ha. What a laugh. You're so funny. I'm starting to enjoy being around you. You are a laugh riot. Almost fainting again." Jennifer can't stop laughing, and Brad is looking at the two of us with a puzzled look on his face.

"Sorry." I'm gasping, but at least I didn't faint. I'm improving.

"At least you stayed on your feet this time. Do you know what makes you get this way?"

With Brad there, I'm petrified he'll tell Jennifer about us bumping into each other, and then where will I be? Jennifer will know I lied and never speak to me again. Or worse, she'll find something to make my life miserable for the rest of the year.

"No, must be nerves or something. I feel better now."

"Jen," Brad moves over to a free computer, "as much as I love to hang around you and your ditzy Freshman friends, I've got this assignment to do, and I'm going to have to do it now. I'll be pretty busy, so no time for any fun now. See you at lunch, okay?"

Jennifer goes into Brad mode and actually bats her eyelashes at him in slow blinks. I'm hypnotized by the way she does this, like she's in a movie in a crinoline hoop skirt, talking with this gorgeous hunk who's going off to fight the Civil War. She gives Brad an amazing cover girl smile then strolls back toward me.

I take deep breaths through my nose and out of my mouth. I've kept my mouth shut, and the day is ahead of me. All of a sudden, I feel like Cher in *Clueless*. She messed up, but she got the guy, too. The bell rings. I gather up my things and meander to the door. I glance back, and at the same moment, Brad turns around, looks at me, and gives me a wink. It's started raining outside, but inside me, it's all sunshine. Hope begins to worm its cruel way into my life. He didn't tell her we had that accident.

I walk through the halls to my next class trying to figure out why he kept it a secret, our secret. Whoopee, I have a secret with Brad! Now the only problem is, if I like him, and he likes me, how do I get Jennifer to stop going out with him? I wonder if she really likes him, or if she's going with him because he's a football player. I decide to ask her at lunch; after all, she thinks I'm a laugh riot, or maybe I'll ask her tonight at her house.

Reality brings me back with a thud. Even if he winked at me, I'll never get Brad Morrow. He didn't tell Jennifer because he's such a nice guy, that's all. I have no way of getting him. Anyway, I'm beginning to worry about what kind of person I am. How can I be thinking about this when I'm staying at Jennifer's, and she's doing all this for me? My bubble bursts, and my empty stomach growls.

There are two more classes to go before lunch. It's Becky's turn to order, and I'm looking forward to Won Ton soup, fried rice, spareribs, and Chow Fun. But also, I might see Brad again, and for some reason, I think that's better than Chinese food for lunch.

Chapter Ten

Becky remembers to order, and when I get to lunch, I see three brown bags and paper plates on the table. Janie's teacher cancelled her class, so she's eating with us. We divvy up the food as fast as we can; the odor is killing me. Is there anything better than the smell of Chinese food? Yes, the taste, and we dig into our portions. I'm in the middle of my Won Ton soup, biting into a wonton when I see Brad and Jennifer at the table across from ours. Jennifer is drinking a bottle of water and eating a green salad, while Brad has the special of the day, pizza, and he's gobbling it like it won't be there in two seconds. I want to check with Jennifer about tonight, so I start to get up from our table.

"Carolyn, you're not finished with your food. Where are you going?" Janie looks at me as if I am committing a sin.

"I wanted to check with Jennifer about an assignment we have in math for Monday. I'll be right back."

"You're getting pretty chummy with her aren't you?" Becky looks at me across the table with her eyes narrowed as she speaks.

"No, she still treats me like toe jam. It's only school related, and we have to study together tonight, too."

"It's Friday night, remember? Aren't we getting together to watch the Friday night TV programs?" Janie reminds me. I remember last year when we got together every Friday with popcorn and goodies at each other's houses.

I should be put up against a wall and shot. How many lies does this make I have told since I started hanging out with Jennifer? Becky and Janie glare at me.

"Carolyn, we've put up with all of this nonsense too long. If you won't be part of our group, then why should we be together?" Becky's lips are tight, and she spits her words at me.

"I agree," Janie adds. "Why don't you change tables and sit with Jennifer from now on, if she'll have you." It's turned into the North Pole in our cafeteria in one minute. Becky and Janie have icicles in their eyes now.

"I'm sorry, guys. I didn't realize this Honors Math class was going to take up so much time. I'll make it up to you. We'll go to the movies tomorrow, my treat." I don't want to lose their friendship, but I don't know if they'll accept my apology. Also, once they see me tomorrow will they ever believe me again?

Becky and Janie get together and discuss my proposition. All of us love movies and better, they won't have to pay a thing. The icicles begin to melt.

"Only if you promise you will never plan anything without letting us know first. We've been together since kindergarten, and we never keep secrets from each other." Becky does the talking for both of them.

"Okay, I promise, but now you know I have to study with Jennifer, there's one other thing. I'm staying over, too. It'll be too late to go home after we're finished. You understand, right?" I feel sorry for them. I'm jerking them around by not telling the truth.

This last statement has both girls staring at me like wounded puppies.

Janie talks first. "You, you're...you're...you're…"

Becky finishes, "…staying over at Jennifer Taylor's house?"

"Only for tonight. I told you why. It's no big deal. I'll see you guys on Saturday. Jennifer and I aren't going to have any fun, and I'll miss you both. I'll call you in the morning, and we'll plan what movie we're going to see."

The bell rings, and I'm relieved. I see Jennifer race out of the cafeteria toward the bathroom. I get up and follow her, dumping the rest of my cold Chow Fun into the garbage on the way. I'm heartbroken about wasting good food, but I don't have a refrigerator and Chinese food left in a locker? Yuck.

"I'll be at gym in a minute. I've got to go to the bathroom," I yell to Becky as I follow Jennifer into the girl's room. She's in a stall already, and we're the only people in the bathroom. I hear retching sounds from the only occupied stall. It has to be Jennifer, but she hardly ate anything at all. How can she do that? She must really be sick. Stomach flu probably.

I hear the sounds of flushing, and Jennifer appears looking a little pale.

"Jennifer, are you okay? Did you catch a stomach virus?"

"Carolyn, won't you be late for gym? Where is your little sidekick, Becky?"

"I told her to go ahead because I wanted to talk to you about this evening. We're still going through with Operation Makeover, right? I have to know which bus to take. Are you taking the bus, or is your mom picking you up again?"

"Of course it's still on. I'll feel better by tonight. Don't worry; this isn't contagious. It's probably something I ate."

I think she's lying, but I can't be sure. Jennifer splashes her face with water, rinsing her mouth, and walks over to the towel dispenser. She dabs her face with one of the cheap paper towels, which are more like sandpaper. She pulls out her lipstick and glides it over her perfect lips.

"Meet me in front of the school like the last time. My mom is picking me up right after school. You better get your stuff after gym. I've already got mine. See you then." She gives me her usual half smile and leaves the bathroom.

I take a few minutes to compose myself. This lying has gotten me all turned around. Lying to my best friends and watching Jennifer lie about her disturbing condition is taking its toll on me. I look in the mirror and feel my stomach rumble and ache. No time for food now. It's gym time, and once again, I'll be seeing Jennifer. Only this time, we have to be in enemy mode toward each other. I dig up my old hatred for Jennifer and stride toward the gym.

The locker room is the usual frenzy of girls in half undress. I spot Becky and get over to my locker to change. Becky is already in her gym clothes, and I throw on mine without caring how I look. My hair must be a mess, and I wonder if my outfit is on right side out. Becky would tell me if it wasn't, wouldn't she?

I decide to check, since I've passed the mirror and can't turn back.

"Becky, do I look okay? I got dressed so fast I'm not sure my clothes are on the right way."

"Yes, you're fine. Wonder what we're doing today."

"I hope it's volleyball. I loved it last time."

"Nope don't think so. I don't see the nets."

"Becky, I'm really sorry about tonight. Are you really angry at me?"

"I have to admit I was pretty upset with you, but you know me. I'm fast to boil, but I'm also quick to simmer down." Becky gives me her usual smile, and I know she's forgiven me. I feel lower than the sole of my shoe now. She's such a great friend. Was I nuts to be friends with Jennifer? This Operation Makeover is starting to get more and more complicated.

"Carolyn, Miss Gaylon is taking attendance. We have to get in line. Let's go."

We've been hanging around on the gym floor near our spots. Now we run over to get in line, but I'm gasping. My breath thing. Good thing Miss Gaylon begins taking attendance, or I might have fainted again. Will I ever learn to just breathe? Note to self. Remember to breathe. You're a moron, Carolyn. This is bad for your health. Go back to the good old days of you and Becky and Janie.

Skip the Operation Makeover tonight and get back to the comfort of your friends.

"Becky, I have to go to the locker right after gym, and I'm not going on the bus with you guys today. I'll call you like I said at lunch, around twelve tomorrow."

I can barely get the words out. My head is pounding now, and I'm gasping for air.

"Carolyn, you're almost purple. For goodness sake, would you breathe? What's gotten you so upset now? I thought you and Jennifer were okay. Aren't you? I can't figure you out anymore."

In and out, through the nose and out through the mouth, I will myself to breathe.

"That's it, you're looking better. Here comes Jennifer. Shhh, Miss Gaylon is coming, too."

"Rebecca Roberts, Carolyn Samuels, Jennifer Taylor. We're finished with attendance, and remarkable for a freshman class, there is perfect attendance."

"We're going to do gymnastics today. Line up in size places behind the mats."

I'm right in the middle, not too tall, not too small. Becky is behind me. She's taller, and Jennifer is behind Becky. She's the tallest of us all. But does Miss Gaylon go by size? Of course not. I wonder why she has us line up like this.

"Carolyn Samuels, come to the mat and do a somersault. It can be any kind, but you must turn over completely."

Becky whispers to me as I creep toward the mat, "It's nothing. Remember to breathe."

I kneel on the mat and try to remember how we were taught to do a somersault in grade school. Kneel down and tuck your head under your arms and propel your body over your head. It sounds easy, but my body won't go over my head. I try again and tuck my head in even further. Finally, after the third attempt, I manage to roly-poly myself over, and the whole gym class is laughing at me. I get up groggy and walk back to my place in line. Jennifer looks at me with a smirk. It won't be hard to hate her. Is she purposely being miserable to me, or maybe she can't believe anyone wouldn't know how to do a basic somersault.

"Jennifer Taylor, please come up here and show the class how a simple somersault should be done."

Jennifer strides to the mat and kneels down. In a second, she has done a perfect kneeling somersault. She gets up and glares at me. I wonder if this is an act or for real? I can't take the not knowing.

"Count off in ones and twos. Then all the ones face the twos. You are partners. Make a double line and start. You have to be able to do this, or you won't pass gym this quarter. Your partner will check to see if you have done it correctly. When you are finished, come over to me. This is the first day of our gymnastics unit. We will be reviewing a few more ways to do a somersault, and you will be tested on these. Ready, begin."

Miss Gaylon goes over to the mats and stands there while we find our partners and form a double line. I realize, while my undigested Won Ton soup begins to repeat on me, I have Jennifer for a partner. Life is playing cruel trick on me lately. Becky looks over at me and winks. She's enjoying my discomfort. Who can blame her? I deserve it. I smile back at her. Our eyes lock, and everything is okay.

"Great, I'm stuck with the gymnastically challenged. Can't you do anything normally? I've been able to do this kind of somersault since I was four. Look, watch me."

Jennifer does a perfect somersault with her body over her head. I kneel down and try. Mine looks like a turtle trying to get itself off of its back; I roll over to one side.

"You've got to do it straight. It's all in the way you put your shoulders on the mat. If you do it right, you can execute it perfectly every time."

"I'll try." I kneel down again and tuck my head under. This time I get my shoulders on the mat before I start to turn over. It works, and I do a perfect somersault. "Miss Perfect" does it again. We go over to get checked by Miss Gaylon, and I do it right one more time. Has Jennifer's perfectness transferred to me?

"If you have been checked on your somersault, you can jog around the gym until the bell rings." Miss Gaylon is going to be nominated most annoying teacher in the whole school soon. Why do we have to run now? Did I have any energy to do this?

Jennifer and I start to run, but soon she forges ahead of me. Is this a race, I wonder? Or am I so slow, she can pass me anytime she wants to? We're halfway around the gym when suddenly I see Jennifer starting to slow down. She stops running and starts to walk. She looks almost white, and I wonder if she is really sick.

"Jennifer, are you okay?" I pass her at a slow trot.

"Just tired I guess. All of a sudden I felt a little faint. Don't laugh. It can happen to anyone."

"Did you forget to breathe as you ran? That could cause it."

"Very funny, Carolyn; did I forget to breathe?"

"I thought it was. Do you need to see the nurse?"

"No, I'm fine, but I'd like to sit down."

"There's Miss Gaylon. I'm sure if you tell her you don't feel well, she'll let you."

"This is funny. Now it's me who needs to go to the nurse, but I'll be okay. Just need to sit down. Once I do, I'll be all right."

Jennifer slows down, and soon she's stopped completely. I look at her, and she looks way too pale. I grab her around the waist and walk her over to the bleachers. Miss Gaylon notices and comes over immediately. Jennifer looks dazed.

"Jennifer Taylor, are you sick? You don't look good at all."

"Miss Gaylon, I think she hurt her foot, twisted her ankle, but she's okay now. I'll stay here and check on her."

"Let me see that ankle. Hmm, it doesn't look swollen. You will be fine in a few minutes. The bell is going to ring soon. You stay there, and in a few minutes go get changed."

"Thanks, Miss Gaylon. I'm feeling much better now."

Jennifer looks at me with surprise and happiness.

"You are always amazing me, Carolyn. I guess I should have eaten a little more at lunch. Now I remember. I got sick after breakfast today, too. No wonder I have no energy. Thanks for helping me. I might have fainted if you hadn't brought me over here."

Across the gym, Becky and her partner are staring over at Jennifer and me. Becky mouths to me, "What happened?"

I mouth back, "She's sick and needs to rest."

"Are your plans off?" Becky keeps miming to me.

"No, she's feeling much better now, must be her period." This is the last lie I want to tell Becky today. All of the lies I have told seem to be lying in a puddle at my feet.

The bell rings for the end of the period, and I race toward my locker. I change in a flash and run down the hallway to my other locker. I grab my books and suitcase, and streak down to the front door. Meanwhile, I scan the halls for Brad. I don't want to bump into him again.

I'm in a fog racing toward the front door. Brad comes from the staircase, and we are separated by a hundredth of an inch. This time we meet face to face in the middle of the front hallway. Jennifer walks out of the gym looking a little frazzled. Jennifer Taylor looking frazzled? The end of the world is coming. Brad sees her and walks straight over like a guided missile.

"Jennifer, you look awful. What happened?"

"Brad, I'm so glad to see you. I felt sick in gym, but it's probably not eating enough for lunch. We had to run, and I couldn't keep going. Do you know who helped me though? She's like my savior—Carolyn. She got me over to a seat, and I didn't even have to go to the nurse. What a girl." She smiles at me. Even better, Brad smiles at me, too.

"Jennifer, it's the least I could do for you," I say. "Now we're even, right?"

"Yeah, I guess we are. See you outside in a few minutes. You're ready I hope?"

"Yes, I zoomed over and got my stuff. How about you? Are you feeling okay now? We could postpone this you know." I keep my fingers crossed.

"No, I'll be fine. You're coming over, and we'll study, okay?"

I look at Jennifer and wonder why she didn't tell him about the makeover.

"What do you mean you're studying? I thought we were going to spend tonight together." Brad sticks out his bottom lip and pouts.

"Tomorrow night, I'll go out with you. Remember, my parents only allow me one night a week for dates."

"Okay, I'll call you tomorrow and see you tomorrow night."

"Thank you, Brad. You do understand don't you?" Jennifer purrs to him, rubbing her hands up and down his arm. Brad puts his arms around her and gives her a big hug. Jennifer gets up on her tiptoes and kisses him on the cheek. I'm way too jealous to continue watching this sappy scene.

I walk outside and try to forget what I just saw. Brad will never like me the way he likes Jennifer. I don't think she cares about him as much as he likes her, but she can sure twist him around her finger. I want to learn how to do that, too. One minute he's angry and sullen, the next he's hugging her. For the fifty thousandth time in my life, I wish I could be like Jennifer Taylor. But not for everything I think. Don't want to have her eating problems.

Chapter Eleven

I push all these thoughts aside when Jennifer comes out of school. Her mom pulls up, and we get into the car. This time Jennifer searches the refrigerator for food. She decides to have a chocolate bar and potato chips. She chats with me on the way to her house as if nothing happened. I doubt she will tell her mother about gym either.

I overeat. She under eats. She gets rid of her food; I manufacture fat. Plus, she has Brad, and I don't. This hurts me so much I want to have some potato chips, too, but I realize eating them won't help me or change my problem. I have a crush on Brad, and he thinks I'm a ditzy freshman, part of Jennifer's groupies. How can I make him change his mind? I think of Operation Makeover as my first step.

"Carolyn, we're starting now." Jennifer's voice bursts into my thinking. "See this food. What do you choose?" Jennifer says as I poke through the basket of snacks in front of us.

"I guess the Rice Krispies bar. It tastes good and is probably not too bad for me."

"Not bad for you, true, but something better is there. Keep looking."

I look through the refrigerator and find a couple of slices of cheese and two apples.

"How about the apple? I could have a slice of cheese, too, if I'm hungry."

"She's right, ladies and gentlemen; the correct answer is apple. A healthy and tasty fruit packed with goodness. Now take a bite, Carolyn, and Operation Makeover will continue."

"What are you going to make me look like? What can you do with this frizzy hair and ridiculous body?"

I'm beginning to think this isn't such a good idea. I'll tell Mrs. Taylor to drop me at home after all. I can call Becky and Janie, and we can still have our night together. But my life is being changed whether I like it or not.

"We'll think of something when we get to my house. I'm thinking you will look very good in straighter hair. So I'm going to wash your hair and put it in rollers, and then we'll look in my wardrobe for things in your size. I have a few clothes in every size up to fourteen; we'll find you an outfit. Then if we have time, we'll practice some tumbling in my gym."

Her gym? Jennifer has her own gym? I'm too dazed to think at all.

I wonder why she has clothes in every size, but I'm thrilled I won't have to buy new clothes. I've been dreading this, but it's not bad so far. Of course, I still have to get through dinner and afterward with Jennifer and her mother. What if her father is there, too?

I have no more time to think because we arrive at Jennifer's house, and I'm whisked up to her room. I've brought my robe to change into, and I do that now, keeping on my underwear. I love my blue terry cloth robe with the white clouds on it. It helps me feel more comfortable, even here in Jennifer's amazing room.

We go into her bathroom, and she has me sit backward on a chair with a thick pink cushion. I put my head on the edge of the sink. She wets my hair under the faucet and pours on shampoo, which smells like pineapple and coconut. Jennifer says it's good for dry, frizzy hair. I like the smell. Halfway through the rinsing, I realize aside from my neck hurting from lying on the cold, hard sink, I'm enjoying this. After the shampoo, Jennifer takes a little handful of this raspberry smelling stuff and spreads it on my hair. I feel like a fruit salad. Just toss me with a couple of cherries.

"Jennifer, how come everything smells like fruit?"

"Shhh, don't ask questions of your makeover artist. Put your head under the faucet, and we'll be done." Is Jennifer being funny?

When she finishes, my hair is soaking wet, and water is streaming down my face and onto my back. Jennifer wraps a towel securely around my head and twists it so it hangs down the back of my head. I haven't felt so pampered since the day before my cousin's Bat Mitzvah when Mom decided we should both go and get our hair done with a manicure and pedicure.

Soon she's pulling a wide toothed comb through my towel-dried hair. It's going through much faster than when I comb my hair myself. *Must be the new conditioner.* I'm so relaxed I could go to sleep, and in no time at all, my whole head is in large hot rollers. I wonder if there is anything she can't do.

"We have about two hours before dinner, and you should be pretty dry by then. But I'm going to keep those rollers in until afterward, so here's a scarf to put over them. My parents won't mind if you show up with rollers in your hair. It's Friday, and we don't dress on Fridays."

What did she mean they don't dress on Fridays? The last time we ate together it wasn't a big deal. Maybe with her father it was different.

"Now we should start thinking about a new wardrobe for you. What is your favorite color? Mine is either pink or red. Let me guess, it's probably blue. Am I right?"

"How did you know?"

Of course any idiot could see mine is blue. I have a blue robe with blue slippers. My book bag is blue, and everything I'm wearing today is blue.

"Let's go to my closet and see what I have. I think I've got the perfect outfit for you. I bought it because it was on sale, but I never wore it. I picked up the wrong size, and it was too late to bring it back when I realized. It's brand new. How about trying it on?"

"I'll try it on if you want me to."

Jennifer opens one of her closets, and I'm blinded by the amount and styles of her clothes. She goes through each item like a careful shopper until she finds the outfit she wants. It's blue all right, blue jeans with tiny dots everywhere. The top matches, but there's only a few dots on the pocket of the long sleeved shirt. Definitely not something I would ever pick out for myself.

"Try it on, and let's see how it looks. Of course you have to imagine your new straighter hairstyle and makeup. But at least you'll see if it fits. I know it's about a twelve."

Jennifer takes the outfit out of her closet, which is ten times larger than mine and consists of two doors, and lays it on the bed. In between the closets, there is a three-way mirror, and I check myself in that one. From any angle, this outfit looks amazing

Of course I don't recognize myself with the rollers in my hair, but I am imagining what it might look like without them. Another amazing thing, the outfit feels a little loose. I make a note to check the size when I take it off.

"Carolyn, you look incredible in this outfit. You must take it. I have no use for it at all. I really hate all blue, but you look terrific in this."

"Do you really think I look good in it? But I do love blue. I'll think about it."

I have decided to take it, but I don't want Jennifer to know yet.

"Okay, now what?"

"Keep trying on different outfits until we find the perfect one. You want to dazzle this guy right? I don't know if this is the one to knock him off his feet."

Jennifer goes back to her closet and moves the clothes around until she stops at another outfit. This one she examines and lays it on the bed. She does this several times until the whole bed is filled with clothes for me to try on.

"Okay, Carolyn, keep putting these on until we find the right one."

I begin with a blue skirt and sweater combination. Then I move onto another jeans outfit with black jeans and a matching top. On and on the fashion show continues with me parading in front of the three-way mirror and then trying on another outfit. We lose track of time, and suddenly I am reminded it is dinnertime by the hunger pangs in my stomach. Today has been a very stressful day, and I've practically eaten nothing. I wonder what dinner will be.

"Jennifer, it's dinnertime," Jennifer's mom reminds us. "We're having pizza for dinner. I hope you like pepperoni, Carolyn. We're pretty casual on Friday nights."

"Thank you, Mom. We'll be down soon. Is it okay for Carolyn to leave the rollers in her hair?"

"Sure, like I said we are very informal tonight, but you will have to put on your clothes. We don't allow anyone to eat dinner in a robe. I hope you understand."

Whoa. That is what she means by casual? In my house, casual means wearing your pajamas or junky clothes.

When did these people ever relax? I can barely think, though, because I'm so hungry. Visions of pizza keep blocking my thoughts, and I get back into my own clothes to be ready to go to dinner. Soon, all I can think is pizza and the cheese melting into the tomato sauce. As we're going downstairs, I'm thinking *pizza, pizza, pizza.*

Jennifer's family eats pizza in a different way than my family. The table is set with china plates, not paper, and a place setting of silverware. Each person has a cloth napkin wrapped in a napkin ring with the letter T on it. A woman comes around and serves us our pizza. It isn't in a box, but on a round metal tray with a pedestal, like in a restaurant. I'm all set to stuff mine in my mouth. At home, no one waits for anyone to eat. But Jennifer takes her knife and fork and starts to cut hers. I can't use my hands because it wouldn't be right to do that. I'd look like a slob. So I cut mine too and eat it with a fork. It doesn't taste the same as when you bite into it, and the cheese gets all stringy and leaves a trail from the slice to your mouth. Here it's very dainty and there are no cheese trails. It's too civilized for me.

Besides pizza, there is a big salad in the middle of the table. I am supposed to help myself, and I do. There are all kinds of dressings, too. I choose the blue cheese, my favorite, and spoon some onto my salad. I watch Jennifer to see how she is eating. She and I are eating almost the exact amount of food. I wait for her to excuse herself at the end of the meal, and I am not surprised when she does leave the table. Jennifer says she's going upstairs, and I should finish my meal. I follow in a few minutes because I don't want her to get suspicious I am spying on her.

I hear the water faucet going, but there's another sound, too, very faint. Was she still sick, or doing this on purpose? How can her parents let her do this? I wonder if they are aware of it and hiding it from me. Or are they so wrapped up in their own lives, they can't see Jennifer, "Miss Perfect," needs help. I realize she is getting worse and worse each day. Why won't she let me know the truth? When will she trust me? These questions burn a hole in my head while Jennifer continues to purge her dinner.

I wait outside the bathroom and since my hair is dry I take out the rollers. Jennifer comes out of her bathroom while I'm unrolling my hair. She doesn't look any different. Her color is good, and she has fixed her hair so she looks perfect.

"Hi, guess I had a bad reaction to the pizza. It's one of the foods I should never eat when my stomach is upset."

I look her in the eye, take a deep breath, and pray I'll be able to let it out again.

"Are you really sick? Or is it something else?"

Jennifer sits on her immaculate comforter with the tiny pink roses, and her eyes fill with tears. I marvel I can make her cry. And to think last year she made me cry almost every day. Isn't life ironic?

Now that I could make Jennifer cry, I didn't want to hurt her. You're such a wimp, Carolyn, I tell myself and sit on the beanbag chair across from Jennifer.

"I wasn't going to tell you. No one else knows, but you caught on that day in the mall, and later after dinner, I knew I couldn't keep the real reason a secret long with you." Jennifer is blubbering now. She picks up the ratty rag doll and hugs it. The tears spill onto her cheeks and run into her mouth so she sputters when she talks.

"I guess I have to tell you about me before middle school. I weighed twenty pounds more than I do now, and I wore a size fourteen. The summer before middle school, I went on a crash diet and lost all the extra weight. Then my body began to change, and all the boys wanted to be around me. By eighth grade, I was really popular, but it wasn't easy keeping off all of the weight. I couldn't resist the fattening things like chocolate and ice cream, so I started to put it all back on. The urge to eat overpowered everything. So I would deny myself until I couldn't hold out anymore, and then I'd eat the food. I knew my gymnastics coach would flip out when he saw I gained even an ounce, but I couldn't help myself. After I binged, I felt so guilty I couldn't keep it inside me anymore." Jennifer takes a tissue and wipes her tears. She stops and takes a breath.

"So I'd make myself get sick by sticking my finger down my throat. I thought I had it together. Eat anything I wanted, then go to the bathroom and get rid of it. I started spending a lot of time in bathrooms. In between, I drank a lot of water to fill myself up and help it come back up faster." Tears begin spilling down her cheeks again. "That's how I keep my perfect body. My parents don't know. Mom thinks I go to the bathroom so often because of how much I drink. My dad is never around long enough to know anything about me, or my life. It's almost too easy."

She looks at me. "There's another reason I can't let anyone know this. My coach will kick me off the team if he finds out. Last year he found out about this girl who was the best gymnast on the team. But he threw her off the team anyway. I have to keep this a secret, or it will be me this year." She takes a deep breath and leans against the pillows on her bed.

I'm stunned by her confession. I don't know why she's telling me all of this. I feel so sorry for her and lower than dirt for thinking I could steal Brad.

"I keep myself from eating by pretending the food is dangerous," Jennifer continues.

I'm too stunned to say anything and listen to her in silence.

"I'll think the asparagus look like dragons because of their strange colors. Or if I cut open the potato, there will be bugs crawling around inside of it. That makes me lose my appetite for the whole meal. You should try it sometime."

My head is spinning from all Jennifer has told me. I realize she has a much bigger problem than I thought, but now I also have a big responsibility. I have to keep this a secret as long as I can. Did I want to be the one to be responsible for Jennifer being thrown off her gymnastics team? *How much stress must she be in?*

"Okay, Carolyn, *E's True Confessions* is over now. So this is only between you and me. You keep this secret, and I'll get you a date with your crush. Deal?" Then just like that she composes herself, and it is like nothing ever happened. "So I feel better now. Maybe we'll talk and then practice some tumbling later."

Okay, she wants everything to go back to normal. What can we talk about? Then I know. Although I've decided to stop trying to get Brad, I'm still curious about how Jennifer feels about him. "Jennifer, how do you feel about Brad? Is he your crush?"

"Brad is like the best looking guy in the whole school, and he's captain of the football team. What's not to like?"

"Yes, but do you really like him, like him? You know; the I-can't-live without-him feeling?"

"Um, maybe, I guess, but I never thought Brad would be my ultimate guy. I can't have a real boyfriend, because I'm going to be an Olympic gymnast. That's why I have to stay so thin." Jennifer's eyes get a faraway look in them. "This summer I was up in the Lake Placid Olympic Training Village for a month. Now I have sessions three times a week here with our local club, and I practice every day with my coach in our gym. We'll go down there to practice tomorrow, maybe. We get weighed once a week, so we all have to keep our weight down. There can't be an ounce too much, or it will affect my performance." Jennifer's face comes alive when she talks about her gymnastics. She must truly love it to do this to her body.

We get back to the makeover, and Jennifer brushes out the rolls. She uses a lot of gels and two kinds of spray. Finally I'm allowed to see my hair, and I love it. It's all shiny and soft looking, and best of all, there isn't a frizz anywhere. I decide to try on the dotted outfit, and with my new straight hair, it looks terrific.

"I'll return this as soon as I'm finished wearing it," I say to Jennifer.

"No, you keep it. I'm giving it to you. I'll never wear it again."

"Thank you Jennifer, that's so nice of you." I wonder if maybe this isn't a bribe of some kind to guarantee my silence.

"Okay, now you have to show me your crush in the yearbook." Jennifer pulls out her copy of last year's yearbook Brad bought for her. *I'm screwed. Who can I choose for my crush?*

I hope someone pops up who will be suitable. We look through the pictures of last year's freshmen, sophomores, and juniors. No one quite fits my idea of a crush until I rest my finger on Jason Wadsworth, III. He will definitely work. He has dark hair and light blue eyes and is crush-worthy, indeed. He's a junior this year and on the football team. So far so good. Jennifer says she knows him and will introduce us. I feel a little traitorous planning to meet a guy I don't like and don't know so I can be near the guy I do like very much.

I'm suddenly very tired. All of this information is too much for me, and I want to go to sleep and forget what I learned tonight. Pictures of Brad float in my head, and I want to close my eyes and see his face all night.

"Jennifer, I'm getting tired. Can we go to sleep?" Then I realize I don't see another bed. "Where do I sleep?"

She opens her closet and takes out a blow up mattress. We get it ready, and soon I'm lying on the carpet next to Jennifer's four-poster bed, almost asleep.

"Psst, Carolyn, are you still awake? You know I've never told anyone about this. Not even Maura, and she's my best friend. But I think I can trust you, right? We understand each other, and first thing Monday, I'm going to introduce you to Jason Wadsworth, the Third. Too bad you can't stay tomorrow, and maybe tomorrow night, we could go out on a double date. I could get Brad to bring him along for you."

Jennifer is probably waiting for an answer from me, but I have none. So I murmur, "Thanks for everything. I'm really sleepy and can't think."

I'm tempted to stay, but I've never gone out on a date before, and I don't even know if I'm allowed to have one. Besides, I promised Becky and Janie we'd go to the movies. I have to go home in the morning, and the thought of going on a date with Brad so near causes me to hold my breath until I start seeing dots in front of my eyes, and I feel lightheaded. *Good thing I'm in the dark,* I think while I let out my breath. Jennifer is probably asleep since I hear snoring from the bed. Phew, I'm glad she didn't see that one.

I'm sleeping on a satin pillow to protect my new hairstyle in a blow up bed on Jennifer's pink carpet. I doze off to the soft hum of the central air conditioning, thinking about tomorrow and the fun I will have with Becky and Janie who seem like my old comfortable shoes after I've tried on all the new shoes I can find in the store. I'm almost asleep when I grasp what has happened. I turned down my first ever, possible date and the chance to be near Brad Morrow. You are so dumb Carolyn. I scrunch under the covers. What will tomorrow bring, I wonder?

* * * *

I feel sandpaper on my cheek and look up to see Jennifer's cat, Cinnamon, licking me. She has pounced on my stomach and is staring at me intently while moving her tongue up and down on my face. A faint vrmm, vrmm sound comes from her; she's enjoying this, but I'm not. Jennifer is still asleep, so I endure the licking as long as I can.

"Cinnamon," I say to the animal standing on my chest. I met her last night when I arrived but forgot about her with all that was happening.

"Cinnamon, can you stop?" I don't have a cat and know very little about the habits of cats. In fact, the only experience I had with cats wasn't great. Once I babysat for someone with a Siamese cat. When the kids were asleep, the cat went berserk. It started to stalk me and moved to the top of the sideboard. Then for no reason at all, except of course to the cat, it pounced on me, and I fled. The cat had sharp claws, and I was terrified of it. After avoiding it for a few minutes, I panicked, scared it would attack me again. When the cat retreated, I left the room and locked it inside the dining room by shutting the door. I tried to watch TV and regain my composure, but I never trusted a cat after that night. So if I have to babysit for people with a cat, I always tell them I'm allergic, so they'll put it far away from me. Now Cinnamon is reminding me of all my fears, except she seems totally harmless.

Cinnamon stops licking me suddenly, like she's figured out I'm not Jennifer and jumps onto the bed to wake her mistress.

"Good morning, Cinnamon, you're up early today, aren't you?"

"Morning Jennifer, she was just licking me; probably thought I was you, huh?"

"Hey Carolyn, how long have you been awake? I think it's too early to get up yet." She turns over and goes back to sleep.

90

But I'm up and decide to do some homework. I don't think I'll ever get over having homework every weekend. The glamour of high school is rapidly wearing off. Along with the fun, there is too much work. I grab my assignment notebook and check my assignments. In history we have to write a diary entry each night for every set of chapters we read. We have progressed from the cavemen to the agrarian societies. Our latest chapters were about the Fertile Crescent and the beginning of agriculture.

I begin reading and soon get caught up with the unfolding of civilization. My diary entry is for a young girl who lived during that time. I'm seriously into writing it, when Jennifer peeks over my shoulder and totally scares me.

"Are you doing work? What a drudge. You even do homework on a Saturday morning. Do you have a life at all?"

"Good morning to you, too, Jennifer. I wouldn't even be up, but Cinnamon woke me thinking I was you, and by the time she realized I wasn't, it was too late to get back to sleep. Don't you remember I woke you to tell you?"

"Oh, that was real. I thought it was a dream. Cinnamon is getting old, and she forgets sometimes. I'm up now, so are you hungry?"

Funny the first thing she thinks about is food. I'm trying to ignore my grumbling stomach, but it's useless.

"Sure, let's have breakfast. What time is it?"

"Why, are you in a hurry? Have a hot date? Ha, ha, ha."

"No, but I promised my friends I'd call them at twelve. We're going to the movies together. What are you doing this afternoon?"

"I'm getting ready for my date with Brad. I'm getting my nails done and a pedicure. Then I'll wash my hair and hang out until it's time."

"Sounds like fun, but I'd rather go to the movies."

"Let's go downstairs and see what Mom has in the kitchen. It's fix everything yourself on weekend mornings. My parents sleep late, and as long as I clean up, Mom doesn't care what I eat."

"Okay, let's go. I'm starving."

We go downstairs and have a huge breakfast. Mrs. Taylor has bought bagels and cream cheese and Danish, and we have orange juice and nonfat milk.

While spreading cream cheese on my bagel, I look over at Jennifer's plate. She has three bagels with cream cheese and a Danish. She doesn't look up as she stuffs each bagel half into her mouth. She's on her Danish, and I'm still on my only bagel. Gulping down an entire glass of juice and following it with a full glass of milk, she barely talks to me. She's a one-girl eating machine. Food is everywhere on her face, and she can barely get one bite chewed before she takes another one. I guess our talk last night has allowed her to be herself with me, because I know she wouldn't act like this in public. Sure enough, suddenly she excuses herself and rushes upstairs. I don't follow her. I can't stop her. My eyes get teary, but I don't know what to do. So I stay downstairs and finish my breakfast. A glance at the clock tells me it's close to twelve, and I have to call Becky and Janie. So I pick up the phone and dial Becky's number. She answers.

"Hi, Carolyn, how's everything? Did you study a lot last night?"

I forgot I told them I was going to be studying. Well, I did kind of study this morning, so it isn't a total lie.

"Yes, but I'd rather have spent the night with you and Janie. What did you guys do? Were the shows fun?"

"Yeah, but we both missed you. Hope you don't have to study every Friday night."

"I hope I won't have to also. Let's go to the movies. I need to relax. Call Janie and tell her to be ready. Can you make a two o'clock movie? I'll get my mom or dad to drive us. I'll give you a call when I get home."

Becky says goodbye, and I hang up. I'm not feeling so good.

Guilt makes my breakfast do somersaults in my stomach. What if they find out the truth? Will they still be my friends? I doubt it. I know I usually won't even talk to someone who lies that much to me.

Jennifer is still upstairs, and I don't want to disturb her, so I clean up the kitchen and waste time reading magazines until she comes back downstairs. She finally returns, moving slowly and looking very pale and drained. Sitting at the kitchen table, she puts her head down. Is she crying?

"Jennifer, are you feeling okay?"

"Yeah, I guess, but I didn't mean to eat so much." She looks a little like a kitten caught lapping up spilled milk. "I can't help myself sometimes. You know I sometimes take whole bags of candy and eat each piece. Then I eat huge bags of chips. I do it late at night when no one is up. I hide the food in my closet. Then I go into the bathroom and stick my finger down my throat. Each time I feel worse, but I have to stay at the right weight. I can never go above it. I want to stop this, but I can't." Looking in her eyes I believe her. "I've tried, but every time I gain weight. Sometimes all I eat for days is salad and juice, but then I have to eat again and start all over." Right now she doesn't look like the public Jennifer at all.

Jennifer's life is too complicated for me. I don't want to know anything more. I don't want to know what I know now. But it's too late. She told me too much about herself. *Jennifer needs to see a doctor.* But even her parents haven't helped her. How will I?

Chapter Twelve

Jennifer's parents get up soon after we finish breakfast, and I thank them for letting me stay over. Mrs. Taylor tells me I can come back anytime. I'm glad she can't read my thoughts.

Jennifer and I go down to her personal gym and practice tumbling on her pink mats. With mirrors on both sides, it is easy to see myself and correct the form as I tumble over and over. Then we try cartwheels, and funny thing, I don't have trouble doing these. Jennifer is a great teacher, and she shows me exactly where to place my hands and how to turn my legs over without looking like a wobbling top. Of course, I am not doing them at any standard to make the cheerleading team.

"Phew, I never did one of those before. Did I look too awful?"

Jennifer sits on the mat watching me. "You're no gymnast, that's for sure. But I think you might be able to do these in public someday," she says with a big smile.

It's not a rave, but I'll take it. Seeing Jennifer smile gives me a warm glow. I almost let down my guard. *What a weekend this has been,* I think, as we head upstairs.

We go back to Jennifer's room to repair my hair, and she smoothes it back to its original shiny style. *How am I going to do this by myself?* But Jennifer assures me it will be easy and gives me the hot rollers.

"I can't take these."

"No, please you can have them. I don't need them for my hair. They're one of those birthday presents I forgot to exchange."

Stuffing them into my book bag I wonder if this is connected to her confession, too.

I have called my parents, and I see Mom's car pull up in front of the house.

"Bye, Jennifer. Have fun on your date with Brad tonight."

"Wish you were coming with us. Hey, how about sitting at our table this week?"

"Only if I can bring Becky and Janie with me."

"Whatever," Jennifer says.

She is really trying to keep this weekend quiet.

Really, though, I'm envious of her, and I feel like a dog staring up at the table waiting for food scraps. Only instead of food I want Brad. I smile at this, and I'm glad Jennifer can't know my thoughts either.

With my book bag over my shoulder, I run to the front car door and jump in. I'm so happy to see Mom. I want to shut out everything I learned this weekend about Jennifer. But it sneaks up like a shadow I will have with me from now on.

"Hi Mom, I'm glad it's you who came to pick me up."

"Wow, you look amazing. Did Jennifer do that to you? I don't remember you telling me you were getting a makeover. Oh, you have on a new outfit, too. I hope you didn't spend any money this time." She turns to me and says, "I know, it's been a tough week for us. At work we're in the middle of this big campaign, and I haven't been home too much. I'm sorry it's been like this since the first week of school." Mom stops and beams at me.

"Well, these are probably the hardest weeks I've ever had in school. High school is much different than I thought."

"What's different? I know you have more homework. You're with your friends, right? You said Becky was in gym with you?"

"Right, but that's the only class. I don't know anyone in any of my other classes except Jennifer, and now she and I are going to be friends."

"That's wonderful, Carolyn. I'm glad you two made up, and it's nice you're getting together. You know Veronica and I have been friends for a couple of years. Jennifer is really a lovely girl. She knows a lot of kids, too. If what Veronica says is true, Jennifer wants to go out during the week on dates. But Veronica feels she's too young for dates during the week. She told me they had a big fight about it."

"I know, Mom. I never thought we would be friends, but I guess we found out we have a lot in common." I take a deep breath. "So I'm going to sit with her at lunch. I haven't told Becky and Janie yet. Do you think they'll want to sit with her?"

"I think that's up to them."

Mom turns into our driveway, and there is my house. No columns, no circular driveway, and its peeling red boards look worse in the daylight. I turn to Mom and hug her. No one is around, and I'm so glad we're spending some time together.

"I've missed you so much this week," I say into her hair.

"Carolyn, I feel so guilty about not being home for you after school. I'll try to be here more often. Would you like that?"

"Yes, Mom. Sometimes I have questions Dad can't answer. I like being with you. It helps me feel better."

"Is there something you want to tell me?"

I pull away from her and sit up straight.

"No, just that I've been a little lonely this month, but I'll get used to it."

Now I'm forced to keep more things from Mom. I want to break down, lay my head in her lap, and cry. Then she'd pat me on the back and tell me everything is going to be all right like when I was little. I feel the tears coming into my eyes and look away so Mom can't see them, and I wipe my eyes with the back of my hand.

"Let's get out of the car. Your father must be wondering why we're not inside yet. Oh, also your friend Janie called and said to tell you she can make it to the movies. Are you going this afternoon?"

"Yes, can you drive us?" I look at her with my puppy dog look, hoping she will feel so guilty she can't resist anything I ask.

"Maybe, I'm not doing anything this afternoon, but I did want to relax. So I won't go with you. I'll just bring you and pick you up."

"You are the best mom ever." I race out of the car and into the house before she can change her mind.

Becky calls when I get into my room. I plop on my bed and speak with her for a few minutes.

"Great, so we'll pick you up in about an hour. Is Janie coming over, or do we have to pick her up, too?" Janie has an art class on Saturday mornings that sometimes runs late.

"She's coming over, because the movie is closer to me."

"Can't wait to see you guys."

"See you soon, Carolyn."

I say goodbye to her and hang up the phone. A wave of good feeling goes through me. I look forward to the movies and put the things I know about Jennifer into an invisible folder in my brain.

My bed feels so comfortable. I stretch out and relax with my head on my pillows. Thoughts about last night creep into my head. I've been invisible for such a long time it feels peculiar to have someone notice me. I haven't decided whether I like Jennifer and me being friends. It's strange to be friends with someone who has taunted me for a year. Why should I desert my real friends, Becky and Janie, for Jennifer? I don't think I can handle any of this. Could we all four be friends? Will Brad speak to me when I start sitting at Jennifer's table for lunch?

A warm glow starts in my cheeks and moves down until I feel all toasty all the way to my toes. Visions of Brad and me talking about how we love pepperoni pizza and me giving up my usual yogurt so we'll both be eating the same thing are better than any movie I'll be seeing today. What will the Brad and Carolyn movie be like? Will it be a romance, I hope? Or maybe it'll be a mystery. Watch and see if the girl gets the boy.

Stop it, I tell myself and bolt upright, hoping to erase the thoughts. Time to get dressed to go to the movies. Time to be the old Carolyn, and I'm looking forward to crawling back into my old life, like an old easy chair. I need to feel like myself again.

* * * *

When Becky and Janie see me, they can't believe it.

"What did you do to yourself at Jennifer's house? I thought you were going over there to study?" Both say almost at the same time.

"We did, but afterward she insisted on doing my hair, and then she gave me this outfit."

"Did you know she was going to do that?" Becky says.

"Why would she all of a sudden decide to make you look so good?" Janie says.

"She has this thing. She loves to do people's hair, and she was giving this outfit away, but I'm the right size, so-o-o…"

"Well you look so great it doesn't matter how or why, so forget it." Janie examines me with her artist's eyes.

"Hey Carolyn, what are we seeing?" Becky's voice eases over me.

I turn to her and say, "Whatever you guys want to see. I don't care. It's my treat, so go for it." They're not upset about my new look at all. I sit back and try to enjoy the day.

"Okay, how about we see the new love story?" Janie leans over and giggles.

"Sure, you know I can't resist them. Let's check it out on your phone." Becky just got a new smart phone as a reward for watching her brothers. "If the time isn't right, we can hang around for the next show. Do you have anywhere to go tonight?"

Both girls shake their heads no, and I think how pathetic we are that none of us has a date for Saturday night. But to be fair, we are only freshmen, and I've never had a date in my life. Don't think Becky or Janie have either. A thought nags at me, I could have a date tonight, and I could have been with Brad, if I had said yes to Jennifer for the blind date with my surrogate crush, Jason Wadsworth III. He's good looking, but looking at his picture doesn't give me prickles head to toe like looking at Brad does.

"Carolyn, we're here at the movies. Have you been listening at all to what I've been saying?" Becky says, nudging my shoulder. Too late I realize I've totally tuned out Becky and Janie while I was thinking.

"What did you say? Sorry, I must be tired from last night. We stayed up pretty late to study." Lie number fifty at least.

"Just wondering about what we'll do while we're waiting if we have to wait. Janie and I were thinking we'd go shopping."

Mom pulls up to the mall where the movie theater is and lets us out at the entrance. I explain we might be later than I thought, and her eyes get wide. She smiles.

"No problem, honey. I'll take a nap, and you call me when you're ready to come home. Either Dad or I will pick you up. Have a great time." Mom gave me money before we left, so I say goodbye, and she leaves happier than I've seen her in a while.

"Let's make sure the times were right for the movie. We can buy our tickets now, too," I say.

"You're the boss; you do remember you're paying for us, don't you?"

"Yes, Janie, I promised, and a promise is a promise is a promise."

"Right, do you remember from that Dr. Seuss book? '*An elephant's faithful one hundred percent.*'" Becky laughs. This was our favorite book in first grade.

"That's me, your old faithful elephant." I laugh, and we stroll over to the movie theater. It's located in the middle of the mall with restaurants on either side of it. When you get near it, you smell a combination of Mexican food coming from La Sol, spicy and mouthwatering, and Asian food from the Asian restaurant on the other side of the theater. I hope the movie time will be right, so we can go into Wok and Roll, the new Asian place.

"Let's look at the movie times, Carolyn," Janie says.

I look up at the movies and times listed on the lighted board above our heads. Our movie is playing in one hour, just as it said. We'll have time to get a bite to eat and shop.

"I'm starved. Didn't have any lunch. Are you guys hungry?" I'm not really hungry, but the aromas are tickling my stomach.

"I can always eat. How about you Becky?" Janie says.

"Why not, are you paying for this, too?"

Mom gave me enough money for the movies and lunch for all of us. I have to do something to make up with both of them. Anyway, while we are eating will be a good time to tell them about the change to Jennifer's table at lunch. I hope they'll both agree to it. Otherwise I don't know how I'll be able to take being at that table with no one speaking to me.

"Let's go to the Wok and Roll," Janie says, moving over to the restaurant as she speaks. "It's right here, and I've always wanted to try it. Okay?"

"Great, but let's buy tickets before we go, in case it's going to be the later show, and we might not get into the movie. That'd be a pain," Becky, always the practical one, says.

"Okay, Becky, I'll buy the tickets, and you guys go to the restaurant. I'll meet you there, if that's okay with you."

I have to get myself ready to break the news to them. But first I need to buy the tickets, so I join the line that formed while we were talking. This is a popular movie, so they're showing it every hour in two theaters. But there is still a possibility we won't get a ticket. So as I inch up to the cashiers, I keep my fingers crossed it won't be sold out before I get to the counter to buy the tickets.

I turn my head and see Maura with one of Jennifer's friends, passing by the movie theater. She's on her cell phone and talking to the girl next to her at the same time.

"Hey, Maura, are you going out with Jennifer and Brad tonight?" Jennifer's friend says.

Maura nods her head.

"Did you hear Jennifer took that dweeb Carolyn home with her last night?" She says to the girl next to her. Then to the person on the other end of her cell phone, "No, I'm gonna have to rush home and change after this. But I just had to get something new for tonight."

The girl with Maura says, "Yeah, she must be doing her part for the wardrobe challenged this week. I mean she spent so much time with her. In school and at the mall, they were all over the place together."

I hope she can't see me, I think as Maura and the girl come into my field of vision.

The girl continues, "I called last night, and Carolyn was over there. She's like her shadow or something."

"Well, she won't be with her tonight when we go out," Maura says and closes her phone.

Damn, she's going out with my surrogate crush. I hope she doesn't turn around and see me. I'd be so embarrassed. She'll know I heard everything she just said.

I'm almost up to the cashier, and I'm about to hand over the money for the tickets when I see SOLD OUT next to the movie name on the board.

"Sorry, this movie is sold out for the three o'clock show. We're selling tickets for the four o'clock show now." One of the uniformed workers is announcing to the crowd.

I hate that person in the uniform. Now we'll have to wait two hours instead of an hour. Oh well, we didn't have anything else to do, and it will give us plenty of time to hang around, shop, and eat. But now we might be here too late and meet Brad and Jennifer with Jason and Maura. Would I be jealous if Maura was with Jason? Or would I have to pretend to be jealous for Jennifer's sake? That would make everything even more complicated, but it's too late to change. So I buy the tickets and head to Wok and Roll.

"Guys, I've bought tickets for the four o'clock show. The three o'clock was sold out. Is that okay with everyone?" I say when I get to the restaurant.

"I guess, because we have no way to get out of here now," Janie says. "

Anyway, I told you I had nothing better to do today," Becky says with a mischievous grin.

I want to hug both of them, because I feel so comfortable, and I hope both of them will always be my friends. But unfortunately, after I tell them what I have to tell them, I'll be lucky if they still want to go to the movies with me.

"So, did you order anything? I'm starved. Now we have a lot of time, and we can really eat."

We choose to go to the market part of the restaurant where we can pick our own vegetables and watch the chefs cook our meal in a wok. First we need to decide what to have, and we all order chicken. So we hurry over to the market, which is full of raw vegetables and all the fixings for a real Asian meal. Then we hand all this over to the chefs and watch as those raw fixings are turned into the delicious meal we ordered.

They toss the chicken into the hot oil, and the sizzling steam seeps toward us out of the small opening where we'll get our cooked meals, and I realize how starved I am. We carry our plates over to the table, and I decide to wait until after we finish eating to tell them. This doesn't help my digestion, though, because I'm too nervous to eat. Imagine that, too nervous to eat! Has that ever happened to me? My brain goes into overdrive, and old memories of eating and me pop up as it sorts through to find the answer to my question—nope, never.

So Becky and Janie start devouring their chicken and vegetables, and I daintily place a few forkfuls into my mouth. In a few minutes, they look up and notice I've still got three quarters of my food left, and I've put down my fork.

"What's the matter, Carolyn? You've hardly eaten anything," Janie says.

"Do you feel well?" Becky, always the concerned one, says.

"Sure, probably not as hungry as I thought before we started eating."

"Seems a shame to waste all this food. Didn't you have to throw out your Chow Fun yesterday?" Janie says as if she were a detective.

"I wonder if you're feeling all right. You never throw out food at all. I think you've caught something," Becky says, putting her hand on my head to check me.

"No, but I've sort of lost my appetite lately. Must be a growing thing or something. Anyway, anyone want some of my food?"

Uh, oh, I'm feeling light-headed. I'm forgetting to breathe. My friends look at me strangely. I feel like a stranger locked outside of a warm house staring through the window at what was once mine. Better come out and say it, or I'll be laying on the floor soon.

"Um, guys, I have something to tell you. You know at lunch how we sit at our own table, and no one talks to us?"

Both girls look up suddenly with questions in their eyes

"Well, on Monday, we're going to share a table with someone else. Believe it or not, she's very nice, but you may not want to eat with her."

"Carolyn, who are you talking about here?" Janie says.

"You have to guess, and you have three guesses."

"Let's see, she's someone we might hate so much we wouldn't have lunch with her?" Again Janie the detective tries to figure out the answer.

"With that description it's got to be Jennifer Taylor. She's the only person I know I hate so much I couldn't even eat with her." Becky gets it, of course.

"You're right, and it won't be so bad."

"You mean like going to the dentist for a checkup and having him fill three cavities at one time?" Becky reminds me of the example she gave me the first day of gym this year.

"Funny, Becky, but I have a good reason for this."

"All right, we're listening, aren't we Janie?"

"Sure, why are we eating with Jennifer Taylor? I'm curious because didn't you have that problem with her all last year?" Janie glares at me.

What am I going to tell them about why we're eating with her? I can't tell the truth, and that makes it worse.

"We sort of made up, and now she kind of thinks of me like her pet. You know she wants to make my life better. So she did my hair and gave me an outfit, and now she wants me to eat with her, because she wants to introduce me to her friends." I'll never get through with this without fainting. "I told her I wouldn't move unless you two were with me. So that's why we're all eating at Jennifer's table from now on." Deep breaths, Carolyn, you can do it.

Becky and Janie look at me like the white coats are coming to take me away in a strait jacket.

"I know what's happened. Aliens have abducted the real Carolyn overnight, and they've replaced her with this replica of her. The replica doesn't know how much Carolyn hates Jennifer Taylor. So maybe we should fill her in?" Becky also glares at me.

I notice their voices are getting harsher, and both girls have stopped eating. They're shooting daggers at me over their unfinished plates of chicken and vegetables. I'd like to slink out of the restaurant and call Mom to get me, but I don't.

"Are you guys really angry at me? I didn't do anything. In fact, I have to tell you once Jennifer makes up her mind to do something there's no way to stop her."

"Carolyn, we're concerned about you. If Jennifer is using you like her own private pet for the week, what is going to happen when she drops you, and she will you know." Becky stops and looks at Janie.

"It won't be pretty I can tell you," Janie finishes.

"Guys, I've got this covered. We'll just go over to the table and eat with her. It'll be fine. You won't have to talk or anything. Plus, we might meet some of her friends. They probably won't even talk to us. But at least we won't be alone anymore." I look back at them with pleading eyes. They turn their backs to me. I can hear whispering.

Becky and Janie turn around with their answer. I see it in their eyes.

"Okay, we'll give it a week. If we feel too uncomfortable, we'll go back to our usual table the following week. Is it a deal?" Becky answers, but Janie nods her head, too.

"Yes, of course. I couldn't imagine being without you two in school. It'd be like peanut butter and jelly without the bread. You're my peanut butter and jelly, and I'm just the bread. We'll always be together, but we can try to have some more friends. Anyway, if we are accepted by Jennifer's group, we're in for the rest of the year. Have you guys thought about that?"

"Of course, we have, and that's why we'll try it. Now let's get finished. I want to go see what they're showing for fall. Maybe I'll get something new," Janie says and gets up to go.

"Yeah, we'll try it. Let's get going. I need to get out there and shop." Becky stands also. So I pay the check, and we leave to wander around the mall until the movie begins.

After going back and forth across three floors, Becky and Janie buy a few CDs, and I get a cleaning cloth for my CDs and lip gloss. We have a lot of fun trying on the new makeup in Sephora. There's a few minutes left, but we decide to go early in case there's a line.

"This'll be fun. We really need more fun, don't we?"

"Yes, Carolyn, we all need some fun and games. How about a video game? Do you have any coins?" Becky turns to Janie.

"Sure, let's go and play some games. We've got loads of time," Janie says, and they walk to the video game section.

"I'll get the popcorn and stuff." I can't concentrate on video games at all, and I buy the popcorn and soda for all of us. I flop down on one of the benches with the tray beside me.

Becky and Janie are immersed in the games. I watch them play but start thinking of Jennifer and Brad together tonight and how really great they look together. I am scum to think of breaking them up. How can I do this to her, especially when she has an eating problem? I'm not really paying attention to anything when I see

Maura pass by the entrance to the movie theater with her friends. She stops and talks with them for a minute and glances into the movie theater. You can look straight into the lobby from the mall since there are no doors.

I almost choke on a popcorn kernel when Maura spies me. She stares, and I look away. I've never been good about returning mean looks.

"Did you see Jen's pet here? She's so pathetic. It's Jen's charity project this year, I guess." Maura looks in my direction and practically shouts so everyone can hear it as she passes. She looks at her friend and laughs as they walk out of the mall.

Becky comes over to me. "Carolyn, won't she be sitting at the table with us? She looks like she hates you. Did you hear what she said?" Becky reminds me when she hears her. Maura was practically screaming.

"I don't know if this'll be a good idea or not, but we promised a week, and a promise is a promise is a promise, as you said before," Janie says, joining me at the bench.

"Where would I be without you guys as friends? I don't deserve you. I'm so lucky."

"I hope you'll remember this all week as we're sitting there waiting for scraps at Jennifer's table. Do you think we should stick out our tongues and breathe hard?" Becky chimes in with Janie at her side. Both of them do an imitation of Max with his tongue out panting.

Janie stares at me sincerely, but all I can do is laugh. She and Becky are making me feel so much better. We go to stand on the line forming by the ticket taker.

The line starts to move, and we get settled into our seats in the theater. The movie is so enjoyable we forget everything. Finally, I have two hours where I can be what I am, just plain Carolyn, invisible with my friends. I'm feeling so much better as we wait for my mom to pick us up at the entrance.

The feeling doesn't last long. We're standing right by Valet Parking when a car arrives, and two couples get out. The driver gets out and gives his keys to the valet. I can't believe it. Then I remember Jennifer said she was going out early, so she could get home for her curfew. It's Jennifer and Brad and, of course, Maura and Jason Wadsworth III. I try to hide behind my friends, but it's too late because they have to go past us. Turning around won't work, because they've already seen my face.

"What do you know? What are you doing here?" Jennifer looks surprised to see me.

"We went to the movies and saw *Only for You*. We loved it."

"That's what we're going to see. I guess we're a little early for the movie. We're going to the seven o'clock show." Jennifer's arm is through Brad's.

"Hi, Carolyn," Brad says to me. I hold onto my friends for support.

"Hi, Brad."

"Eat any pepperoni pizza lately?" He remembers we both love that. I'm shocked he did.

"Um, no, we went to the Asian restaurant. Have you been there yet?"

"No, but if you liked it, we should try it."

I'm beyond shock now. Brad is going to follow what I did? I will walk on air for the rest of the night. Maybe I'll feel this way all weekend. How great!

"Brad, isn't it time we got into the theater? We might need to get tickets, so we won't miss the movie. Maura, didn't you say there were lines in the afternoon?" Jennifer says.

"Yes, it was sold out for the three o'clock show. That's why I said we should buy the tickets online, right Jason?"

Now I look at Jason, and yes, he is cute in person, but next to Brad, he's a poor second. I start to get that uncomfortable unable-to-breathe feeling, and I hope they'll go inside soon before I topple over in front of Brad. He's so yummy I can't catch my breath. Oh, no, spots start to form in front of my eyes, and I grab onto the steel banister to hold myself up.

"Are you doing that thing again, Carolyn?" Jennifer looks at me suspiciously.

"Must be my allergies, I guess. I'll be fine."

"We have to go in now. See you on Monday. Did you know Carolyn and her friends are joining us on Monday for lunch?"

"See you on Monday, then." Brad smiles at me, and winks.

I sway and hold onto the banister more tightly. Becky and Janie hold me up. Brad and Jennifer go up the stairs with Maura and Jason, and I finally breathe. Wow, I almost fainted. How will I get through lunch without losing consciousness? I'm glad this week is over, but thinking about next week is causing me even more stress. My lies have lies. Don't want to think about eating with Brad. I pray I won't do something stupid in front of him. Also, I wonder if I can trust Jennifer. Can I find a way to help her with her problem? Suddenly, there are too many questions for a Saturday night. All I want is to go home and forget it all. Monday's not here yet. But what will this week bring?

Chapter Thirteen

Monday arrives with a blast. I'm practically thrown out of bed by a clap of thunder. Outside the rain pelts Mom's roses and leaves puddles on our driveway in the hollows Dad always says need to be filled. Max has been sleeping near my bed, but the thunder wakes him, and he pads over and pushes his head onto the bed staring at me, checking to see if I'm okay. I glance at my closet and breathe a sigh of relief. I don't need to be Jennifer's fashion clone this week. Cheerleading tryouts start in a few days, and I picture a brand new cheerleading outfit hanging there with the pom-poms—a matched set. A few girls have quit the team, so they're looking for more cheerleaders. Mom and I went to the doctor last week, and I got a physical so I'd be ready.

Grabbing a pair of jeans and a top I haven't worn yet, I throw on my clothes and spend the rest of the time imagining what it would be like to be a cheerleader at the football game this Saturday. Would Brad notice me? I close my eyes and say over and over: "You can do it Carolyn; you're good at it."

Now all I have to do is believe this. My jeans are practically falling off, so I get a belt before I leave my room, and I'm threading it through the belt loops on my way downstairs, when I hear the phone ring. Who could be calling me so early, maybe Becky or Janie wanting me to give them a ride?

"Carolyn, Jennifer's on the phone." Mom hands me the portable phone.

"Hi, Jennifer, what's happening?" Good thing she can't see my mouth is hanging open.

"Carolyn, we have a minor crisis today. Mom went early to help Dad with his campaign, Brad's car is in the shop, and I just missed the bus. Could you and your mom come by and pick me up? You remember where I live, right?"

"What about Maura, doesn't her mom have a car?"

"She's angry at me, because Jason told Brad he'd never go out with her again. So she wouldn't take me to school. Don't you think I called her before I called you?"

"How did you know I'd do it for you? We're not really friends. You got Maura a date with Jason, and that made me feel lousy when I saw you on Saturday night."

"You told me you couldn't go, what was I supposed to do? Please give me a ride. I'm kind of desperate, although I hate to admit it to you."

"Of course, Jennifer." I hold my hand over the receiver and wish Becky and Janie were here so I could tell them. I've got to call them as soon as I hang up. Do I have time, I wonder?

"See you in ten minutes."

"Hate to say it, but thanks. You know, you do come in handy now and then."

I hang up and call Becky.

"Morning, I know you have only a few minutes, but I had to call you. Jennifer called me for a ride this morning."

"Wow, she must be desperate for a ride to call you. Isn't she friends with Maura? What happened there?"

"Can you talk, or should we talk in school? Don't know when with Jennifer around me 24/7, but how about in gym? She never pays any attention to me there."

"Great Carolyn, now I have to wait all morning to hear about Maura and Jennifer. Can't you tell me now? Damn, there's my bus. Guess I'll have to go. See you in school."

"Cool, you'll die when you hear why. It's so sleazy actually. I can't believe she did it myself."

"You better tell me, or I'll never talk to you again, at least not today." Becky laughs and hangs up. I put down the phone and run into the kitchen. Mom is in her usual place with the Sunday Times crossword puzzle. When she can't work on it during the weekend, she finishes it on Monday.

"There's milk and cereal for you and don't forget to have your orange juice."

I mean she doesn't look up from her crossword puzzle, but she knows I'm there. How does she do that? Maybe when I'm a mother someday I'll find out. Meanwhile, I've got to get Mom going.

"Mom, we've got to leave now. Jennifer asked if I'd give her a ride. She missed the bus, and there's no one to take her. Can we do it? Otherwise I guess she'll have to take a taxi to school."

"Yes, Carolyn, so hurry and eat something, and we'll go."

"That's what I love about you Mom, you never say no to anyone when it comes to anything. But this is the last time you'll hear that from me. If you want to hear it again, you'll have to beat it out of me." Mom smiles and puts her coffee cup in the sink. I gather up my book bag I've started keeping near the back door, pat Max on his huge head, and open the door. We race to the car, and soon we're at Jennifer's house.

We pick up Jennifer, and my day changes completely. Jennifer's face looks pale as if she put on white make up before she left her house. Her eyes have dark circles underneath them, and she slumps into the car totally unlike the person I know.

"Jennifer, you look awful. What's wrong?" I'm almost afraid to ask. How can she go to school this way?

I tap Mom on the shoulder and ask her to pull over to the side of the road. Getting out and going to Mom's side, I ask her to step out of the car. She looks at me as if I asked her to run a red light, but she does it.

"What's so important we have to stop and discuss it here in the middle of the street?"

"Mom, did you look at Jennifer? She looks really sick. Did you see her eyes?"

"I confess I wasn't looking when she got into the car. Let me see her now."

Mom walks over to the passenger's side of the backseat and opens the door. Jennifer tries to greet her with a smile, but it's a useless attempt. She barely takes up a half of the seat.

"Jennifer, are you feeling okay? Why were you late?"

"I have a little upset stomach, Mrs. Samuels. I was in the bathroom until now. But I have to go to school. Can't miss today, it's really important I be there."

"I don't think you should go. Can you call your mom? I think we should take you back home."

"Please don't, Mrs. Samuels. My mother will kill me. I've already stayed out too much last year, and she'll ground me if I get any more detentions because of lateness. Then my coach will bench me, and I won't get to be in the big meet. Please don't take me home. I feel much better now. I'll go to the nurse when we get to school. I promise."

Mom stands there half bent through the back seat door and shakes her head back and forth.

"What do you think, Carolyn? Should we take her to school or back home?"

She would ask me and get me into it. I don't know what to say. I can't risk getting Jennifer angry with me. My life in school will go back to the hell it was last year. I'm kind of getting used to her being friendly to me. Don't want to go back to the old routine. I think I know why Jennifer is looking like this.

I whisper something in Jennifer's ear.

"Yes, yes, that's what happened. All of a sudden it's gotten out of control. I can't stop myself anymore. I can't even eat a slice of bread without doing it." Jennifer looks like she's about to cry, in public, with my mom standing there.

"Mom, I think Jennifer should go to school. I'll take her straight to the nurse. Right?"

Jennifer looks up at me with a thank you in her eyes, and Mom goes back to the driver's seat. I get in and sit next to Jennifer. We continue to school, but now I have a lead weight to carry with me all day. I hope she'll go to the nurse when we get to school. I think Jennifer needs to see more than the nurse. She needs a doctor.

I sit trying to breathe. In and out, easy, slow, take your time. Breathe, Carolyn, breathe. It wouldn't be cool to faint on the way to school; Mom would know for sure about my breathing problem. I'd be busted. As I'm remembering to breathe, I realize something. Both of us have a secret. I'm keeping Jennifer's secret, and she's keeping mine. I glance over at her, and she looks like a scared kid waiting in the dentist's office. She's really afraid this time.

For the first time, I think of Jennifer as one of the kids. The aura she has always had around her has disappeared for the moment. If I were with Becky or Janie and one of them looked like Jennifer did, I'd reach over and put my arm around her. Can't do that with Jennifer. Though her shine is gone, I know it's just temporary. Anyway, maybe she's like Cinnamon, and she'll scratch me if I try that.

So we sit in silence for the rest of the ride, mulling over all the possibilities that have popped up because of this moment.

Chapter Fourteen

"Cheerleading tryouts are going to start this week. Anyone who is interested should come to the small gym after school. Tryouts won't start until tomorrow, but you have to be there for the practice today, or you won't be on the list. Only the first twenty will be accepted. So be there on time and learn the cheers. We can't wait to see all of you."

Announcement time ends, and I look around me. Back in math class and starting a new week. Mr. Armbruster goes over the old homework and gives us the new assignment. So far it's all review. I don't need to pay attention, so I turn my mind to the more pressing problem. Jennifer. When we got to school, I took her to the nurse. The nurse took one look at her and began doing medical things like taking her temperature, holding her wrist, and taking her pulse, and asking her questions at the same time. She wouldn't let her leave with me, so I came straight to math without stopping at my locker. Didn't want to be late for anything.

John, the cute guy, is trying to get my attention. A month ago, I would have practically fainted from this. But now, I know why. He can't be interested in me. He probably misses Jennifer.

I'm right. He starts mouthing a question to me while Mr. Armbruster is answering someone's question about the homework. I don't really understand him.

"Psst, Carolyn, where's Jennifer? Did she come to school?" He leans over and whispers to me.

"She's in school, but at the nurse." I answer him in a voice slightly above a whisper.

"Nurse? Is she sick?" This guy doesn't give up, does he?

"Don't know. Don't keep talking to me. I'm missing what the teacher is saying. You'll get me in trouble."

"Aren't you friends with her? I mean after your project, you two looked like buddies to me." He grins and turns to look at me more closely. I can't be sure, but it seems like he might be sizing me up. It's like he's noticed me for the first time.

"Class, today we're having a little quiz. I'm handing out the papers now. Put your name on it and begin."

What a day. Now we're having a quiz, on a Monday. Does this teacher have no compassion for people? My paper gets to me, and I put my name on top. It's a review of what we did last year. I take my stomach out of my mouth. It's probably fairly easy.

I'm right again. Two out of two. I know all of the answers and how to get them.

Getting finished early gives me a chance to think about my morning. I have to invent a word to describe this morning. It's like Jennifer's morphed into a new person. I have no idea what to think. I find myself actually worrying about her. She's not my friend, but we're tied in so many ways we're something. Best enemies—is there such a thing? I feel sorry for her and practically gag. How can I be feeling sorry for someone like Jennifer? She gets everything she wants, and she has the cutest guy in school. Why isn't she happy?

Mr. Armbruster collects our papers and assigns some problems on the board to do in class.

"You can work on these with your neighbor, but each of you will hand in a paper at the end of the period."

"Psst, Carolyn." John is trying to get my attention again, so I turn to him.

"Now what? Do you want to know what's wrong with Jennifer? How about her home phone?" John never stops.

I'm tired of being bothered by him, but I'm also kind of liking the attention.

"You know, you're tougher than you look. I'm surprised."

I am surprising myself. Where is all of this courage coming from? I think to myself maybe it would be okay to be nice to John. After all, he hasn't done anything wrong except be friendly to Jennifer, and now I'm kind of friendly with her, too.

"Do you want to work together on these problems?" I ask John, since he's got this hangdog expression on his face. He looks kind of lost. I know that feeling very well.

"Are you sure? You haven't been exactly cool to me today." John answers me with a puzzled look.

"Well, I'm sorry if I came off that way, but I've got a lot on my mind."

"Hey, don't we all?"

I see he looks like he needs help, so I move my desk over and continue to do the problems.

"Let's work on these, and then we can talk if you want to. Do you need help with them?"

"Don't know. I haven't started. Wow, you've got three of those done already? Let me do a couple first." He begins doing the problems, and I'm finished before he gets to the second one.

"Geez, how can you do those so fast? Maybe I'd better compare our answers."

He looks at my paper and realizes his answers aren't the same. I recheck my paper and get the same answers. John is erasing his.

"I must have made a mistake somewhere. Let me see what you did. Right, I goofed on the second part. Thanks Carolyn. Now I know where to go if I need an A on a test." He sees my expression.

"Just kidding. Armbruster probably has video cameras hidden all over the room."

I laugh. John isn't bad without Jennifer around. I don't feel anything like I feel for Brad for him; he's a nice guy though.

"So what's a smart girl like you worried about? You can breeze through this class." John looks at me with a question in his eyes.

"Do you really want to know?"

"Sure, but first let me finish these problems and check them with you." He works for a few minutes, and when we check them together, he's got them all right.

"Thanks, Carolyn. If Armbruster calls on me, I'll have them right. You've saved me. Now what's on your mind?"

I sift through the many problems I have. Can't tell him about Jennifer, or my crush on Brad, or lying to my friends, or how I feel about my body. Come to think of it, what can I tell him? I'm not liking myself very much lately; I wish there was a way to go back to the day before school and change everything. Like I could time travel and make everything okay.

"Well, I'm kind of nervous because I'm going to cheerleading tryouts today." I figure this is pretty safe to tell him.

"You don't seem the type to be a cheerleader. Now if you told me Debate Club or the newspaper I wouldn't be surprised. But cheerleading? You're too smart to be one of those airheads. Yeah, they've got great legs, and I love to see them jump, but didn't figure you for one of them. "

"Why? I know. I'm too big, aren't I? You don't want to hurt my feelings, but that's the reason, right?" I feel the tears building, and I know I'm going to make a fool of myself and cry in front of him. Also, unconsciously, I'm holding my breath and only realize this when the room starts spinning.

"No, that's not the reason at all. You look great. I never noticed you with Jennifer here, but you've got no problems at all." He gives me a crooked smile. "No, it's 'cause you've got brains."

Phew, I take in a breath, gulping for air. Without John noticing, I pretend to pick something up from the floor. Did I hear him right? He thinks I look good enough to be a cheerleader? Maybe he's got a vision problem. Or maybe a good witch has cast a spell, and I'm transformed into a beautiful princess. Like the Frog Prince, only I'm the Frog Princess. Turned from a toad into a princess. By what magic? You're an idiot Carolyn.

"Okay, time's up for problem solving. How many of you worked on these together? I was walking around the room and saw quite a few of you sharing answers. I hope you also did the work. Who wants to give the answer to the first problem?"

About four or five people raise their hands, and Mr. Armbruster sends them up to the board to write their answers. All of them have the same answer, and I check mine. It's the same. John looks at me and gives me a thumb up.

"Erase those, and let's have four more go to the board with the second answer."

We continue like this for the rest of the period, and at the end of the period, John turns and smiles at me.

"Carolyn you're a lifesaver. All my answers were right. Good luck on your tryout today. Come to think of it, maybe someone with brains is what this school needs out there."

"Thanks, but we're only learning the cheers today. Tomorrow is the big day."

"What do you say to a cheerleader? Break your pom-poms?"

I giggle. John is really funny. Then I gulp and realize today is the day we move over to Jennifer's table. Three more classes and then lunch. My heart leaps, and I wonder if it's possible to have a heart attack at my age.

"Where are you going in such a hurry?" Becky says to me when I practically knock her down in the hall outside the lunchroom.

"I'm starving, aren't you? Don't know where we're sitting today. If Jennifer's not at the table, we're staying at our old place. I couldn't face her table without her being there."

"Carolyn, what are you talking about? Where's Jennifer, and why wouldn't she be there? I saw her a few minutes ago, and she looked fine. She was with her groupies and Brad."

Whoa, I thought she was so sick she was in the nurse's office all morning. Well I guess she felt better, and they let her go back to classes. Don't want to see her at lunch. My life was so simple when it wasn't involved with hers.

* * * *

Becky and I enter the lunchroom, and we're bombarded with the tuna fish-meatloaf smell and the din of usual lunchtime noise. Jennifer smiles at me as we approach the table. I breathe in and out as I examine the members of her group.

"Everyone, this is Carolyn; you know her. And this is Becky. Carolyn and her friends are sitting with us this week. It's kind of an experiment, so say hi and make room for them."

"Hi." Brad grins at me and moves over to give me a place to sit. We grab a few chairs from the adjoining table and squeeze into the space. The sound of my heart is almost as loud as the lunchroom. Pound, pound, pound. It's like a basketball against my chest. I can barely sit still. I try to eat quietly and be invisible, but I didn't count on Maura.

"Jen, are you slumming today?" Maura looks at Becky and me with a frown like we're ants at her picnic. She wasn't there when we got to the table.

"It's like this Maura. Carolyn has been a big help to me, and I've decided to reward her with a week at our table. If you don't like it, you can move. Otherwise take your seat and eat your lunch. We're all cool with her being here, aren't we?" Jennifer looks each person in the eye, and they all nod yes in unison. I wonder why everyone is listening to Jennifer. She's a freshman, and some of the people at this table are juniors. How does she do it?

I start to spoon some of my blueberry yogurt into my mouth. Maybe food will make me feel better. I notice Jennifer has her usual salad and a bottle of water. She doesn't seem to be eating anything at all. Her face is still a little pale, but she has all her makeup on, and her eyes look much better than this morning. Brad is next to her eating a huge slice of pepperoni pizza. The gooey cheese and the pepperoni are too much to resist. Why couldn't he be eating something I can't stand like the awful meatloaf stinking up the lunchroom? I glance at my watch. Time has taken this moment to go on vacation. Has it only been five minutes?

"Carolyn," Becky pokes me in the ribs and whispers. "When can you tell me about what you told me this morning?"

"Gym," I whisper back to her. She gives me the okay sign and scrapes her spoon into her yogurt.

So far no one has talked to us since Jennifer introduced us at the beginning of lunch. This might not be as bad as I thought. I can handle this, especially with Becky here. I give Becky a smile, and she smiles back. Lulled into a kind of peace, I am not ready for what happens next.

Chapter Fifteen

I'm not paying attention to Jennifer at all, so I don't see the incident until it is too late. All of a sudden people are crowding around her. Why? I wonder and get up to see. The girl who greeted me and Becky has turned chalk white, and her head is resting in her salad. Dressing coats the ends of her perfect blonde hair and drips down onto the table. I run over to her and cut through the crowd watching her with panic on their faces. Brad picks her head up out of the salad.

"Get the nurse, quick," he shouts. "Jen, Jen, answer me. Can you talk?" Brad holds her head and gently cradles it in his arms. Almost as soon as he calls for the nurse, she runs into the lunchroom. I have never seen an adult run in this school before. The nurse zooms over to the table and tells Brad to lay Jennifer on the floor. She takes out her stethoscope, checks Jennifer's heart, and places two fingers on her pulse.

"Never should have let her out of the office," she mutters. "I knew this would happen. I've got to call her parents again. Why don't those people ever answer their phones?" She tells someone to ask the principal to come to her office. Then she turns to the crowd gathered around our table.

"Everything's all right," the nurse tells the huge circle which has formed around Jennifer. "You can all go back to eating. She'll be fine." The nurse asks Brad to get the wheelchair she left by the door. Before I know it, the nurse and Brad are wheeling Jennifer out of the lunchroom.

I get this funny empty feeling when she leaves. I'm actually worried about her. The girl has gotten into my head. Damn, I might actually like her. How can that be? She's been such a snake to me. And, that Maura, oooh.

"Becky, I think I'll go see how Jennifer is before gym. Do you want to come?"

"Nah, you go ahead. I need a little more time to change anyway. It's that time of the month for me."

"Gottcha, I'll be there soon. If I'm late, tell Ms. Gaylon I had to take Jennifer to the nurse. She'll probably get a big kick out of that. "I laugh.

"Yeah, should at least get her to crack a smile. Boy that woman is a pickle."

"See ya later, Becky. You know it's weird. Though Jennifer was so mean to me for so long, I've kinda gotten used to her. It's like when you have a blister on your heel, and it goes away. You kind of miss the worrying about it. Is that sick? Do you get it?"

"Sure, whatever; see how she is. She was kinda nice to us today before she collapsed in her salad. I wonder why she did that. Oh well, it's off to gym. See you later." Becky turns and moves away, and I go in the opposite direction to the nurse.

My head feels like a tossed salad. So much is inside, and I'm so mixed up, I don't know what to do. But my stupid brain won't let me think. All I can see is Brad and what a great thing he did helping Jennifer. Does she really deserve him? Life is so unfair.

Brad is slumped in a chair when I get there. Jennifer's lying on one of the fake leather beds, and she's whiter than whipped cream. Her eyes are half open, and she looks worse than this morning. I creep over to the bed and wonder if she is awake. She gives me a kind of smile and closes her eyes.

"She's okay, just seems really tired. Her parents are coming to get her. The nurse won't let her leave without their signature. I told her I'd take her home, but the nurse wouldn't let me. Has to be her parents. So I'm waiting here. You have to get to class, don't you?" Brad is standing over Jennifer with a look like he just blew a touchdown pass.

"Um, yeah, but, I…I…I …" Oh no, finish your sentence stupid. It's my nightmare coming true. "I…um…stopped by to…um…see how she is." Yes, I'm able to get out a whole sentence to him even though I sound like a little kid.

"Sure, I'll tell her you came by to see her when she wakes up. Now she's resting and kind of half asleep. I got permission to hang out here. Do you want me to let you know when she wakes up? What class are you in now?"

"Yeah, that'd be...um great if you would. I'm at gym now. Might be a problem though. Try anyway, if...um you can." Phew, this is hard work. I'm starting to feel puddles of sweat rolling down from my armpits. I have to get out of there before I drip on the floor in front of him. Too gross.

I race back to the gym to tell Becky about Jennifer, and on the way, I try to think of some way to make up to her and Janie for all the rotten things I've done to them without their knowing it. The guilt from these weeks is like sacks of sand I carry each day. And now, it's like I can't move another step without telling them the truth. But what will they say when they find out I've been lying to them? Will they even talk to me again?

"Carolyn, where are you going? Isn't this your locker next to mine?" I've almost walked past my own locker I'm so lost in this maze. Good thing Becky's here, or I'd have walked into gym completely dressed. Becky nudges me and says, "Aren't you going to open it and get your gym clothes on?"

"Right, I'm sorry, I'm kind of out of it. Thanks Becky. You're such a good friend."

"Now don't go getting all sappy on me. What's with you today? By the way, how's Jennifer? Do you know what's wrong with her?"

"I saw her lying down in the nurse's office. She looked spacey. Didn't even recognize me. But Brad..." I trail off thinking how amazing he is to sit by her until her parents came. He must really like her. There go my chances. *Carolyn, did you ever think seriously he would ever want you over Jennifer? Be real. He'll talk to you, but it's Jennifer he wants.* My stupid mind refuses to accept this. A little chink of hope appears out of nowhere. I remember when we got all tangled the day I almost missed the bus, his expression when he saw me and how it felt to be next to him. Prickles happen all over my body, and I start to breathe funny.

"But Brad did what? Oh, no, are you getting that breathing thing again? Come on breathe in and out, nice and slow, that's right. Okay, your face is back to normal color again. What's wrong with you now?"

"Becky, there's so much wrong I can't begin to tell you, but you are the best, just know that." My breathing is back to normal, and I look at Becky with her smiling eyes and make a deal with myself. I won't think of Brad anymore today. He belongs to Jennifer and that's that.

"Are you ready? It's time for gym."

"Yup, let's go. Maybe there'll be volleyball again today."

"Do you remember the thing you wanted to tell me about this morning? What was it?"

I search my brain for what happened this morning. It feels like a week ago now. Then I remember, that's why Maura was so snippy at lunch.

"Do you remember on Saturday night when we were waiting at the mall, and Jennifer and Maura came by with Brad and his friend? Well Jennifer needed me to give her a ride today, because she missed the bus. She always gets a ride from Maura, but today she didn't because Maura is mad at her."

"Why, what happened, and what does it have to do with Saturday?"

"Maura went out with Brad's friend Jason, and Jason told Brad he never wanted to go out with her again. So Maura got mad at Jennifer. I guess for telling her or whatever. What did she want her to do, lie?"

"I wonder why he didn't want to go out with her, maybe because she's the most obnoxious girl in the school," Becky says laughing. "I can't understand how Jennifer can even stand her. I've never seen that girl crack a smile."

"I don't know either, but they've been friends since elementary school, and I guess she might have changed."

"Whatever, but that is certainly juicy. Who's the guy again? He looked cute when we saw them."

"His name is Jason Wadsworth the Third. He's Brad's friend. I heard her talking about the date when I was over there. He's available if you want to meet him."

"Carolyn, I don't know. He's a junior, and they're so much older and expect more. Me, I've never even been out on a date. Have you?"

"Of course not. But knowing Jennifer, maybe I could get you a date with him. Would you like me to try?" Maybe this would make up for the rotten way I've treated Becky.

"Maybe, but not alone and not just with Jennifer, or I'll tear out my hair. How about if she gets a date for you, too?"

Oops. Now I've really goofed. I should be the one going out with Jason, because I told Jennifer he was my crush. Maybe we could work out something here.

"Becky, maybe Jason Wadsworth the Third isn't your type. Should I see if Brad has other friends? I mean he's on the football team, right?"

"If you think so, but they have to be as cute as Jason, or I won't do it. And you have to come with me, too."

Ms. Gaylon starts the gym period, and there's no more time for talk.

After gym, I tell Becky I'll call her, and I'm getting a ride back home because I have to stay for a study class in math. Another lie, and the sand bags are getting heavier and heavier. I go back to the gym for the cheerleading practice and find a long line outside the door. I count the people and realize I'm the nineteenth person. Just in time. They open the gym doors and start letting us in one by one. Three girls in cheerleading uniforms are at a table set up in the middle of the gym floor.

"Hi, everyone, glad to see you could make it to our practice session today. There should be twenty of you, so would you do me a favor and count off starting with you at one."

The count starts and continues until I have to say, "Nineteen." There's one more girl behind me and a few who are outside the door glaring at us because they can't get in. I see Maura is the last girl behind me, but I ignore her.

"Great, now please come up and sign your names on the sheet. After that, go stand anywhere on the floor."

When all have signed, the head cheerleader, or I guess she is the head cheerleader, since she didn't introduce herself yet, tells us to line up in two lines of ten across the gym floor. I stay toward the front, so I'll be able to see all the steps.

"Hi, again, my name is Mary, and I'm the head cheerleader. You're all here today so we can teach you the steps. We're going to start slow, and if you need to ask a question, wait until we've shown you all the steps. We'll answer them after we're finished. We're going to show you a whole cheer, and then we'll break it down for you." All of the cheerleaders line up facing us with their pom-poms and begin the first cheer

"Buns in the oven, chicken on the grill,

What is the team that gives us a thrill?

Mill Valley, Mill Valley, Mill Valley.

Yay, Mill Valley."

While they are cheering, they do a basic step-step-kick-kick, then step-kick-step-kick, and they all jump up and land with their feet apart. Then they jump, put their legs together, and throw their hands in the air waving their pom-poms. I can do this. I know this cheer. I've been practicing it every day in front of the mirror. I hope I don't trip in front of all these people. It doesn't matter. I know I won't get in. One look at my thunder thighs tomorrow, and I'll be out. But for now it's fun to learn and pretend.

We practice for at least an hour, and I think I've got all the steps down. Then we get into pairs and practice some more with a partner. Finally, we're put into groups of five and practice in front of the cheerleaders. When everyone has the steps, we all show the cheerleaders how we look doing the cheer. The whole gym resounds with the words of the cheer, and we step, kick and jump, waving pretend pom-poms.

I'm hot and sweaty when we finish, so I decide to change my top before I go outside. Did I leave anything in my gym locker I can wear? While I search for something, I hear Maura's voice. Right, I saw her behind me, but I ignored her. Now, she creeps up on me and stares at me like I'm some dirt on her spotless sneakers.

"Look who's trying out for the cheerleaders. Do you think you'll be able to fit into the uniform? I don't think they make them in plus sizes."

I try to ignore her words and realize as Mom always says to me, to consider the source.

"Hi, Maura, are you trying out, too? You know I went to see Jennifer in the nurse's office. I didn't see you there. Isn't she like your best friend?" Maura stares blankly at me. "Oh, and I remember this morning you wouldn't give your best friend a ride. Jennifer had to call me to ask for one." I stare her in the eye and try a mean glare. She gives me a little smirk, and I continue, not sure where this is going. "You'd better be careful, or you won't be part of the chosen crowd anymore. Jennifer isn't even my friend, but I went to see her before gym." Yes, I put the knife in and wiggled it, too.

Maura stands there, staring at me like I'd slapped her. I guess she didn't expect I would say anything to her. I'm sick of her little nasty remarks and how she treats people. With a big grin, I pull my sweatshirt over my head, grab my book bag, and yell over my shoulder, "See ya."

Chapter Sixteen

In two seconds, I'm outside the school and realize I have about half an hour to wait for the late bus. I sit on the curb and take out my homework. I'm doing my homework with my feet in the roadway when I see a car coming towards me. It stops about a few feet from me.

"Carolyn, what are you doing here?"

Oh my God, it's Brad. The one person I didn't want to see. I thought his car was in the shop. He gets out of the car and comes over to me.

"Hi, I had to stay after school for the cheerleading practice. I'm waiting for the late bus. Jennifer told me your car was in the shop."

Wow. I've gotten out three whole sentences without stammering. It seems easier to talk to him now. I mean it's okay if I don't look him right in the eye. Then I have that same problem. It's too intense that way.

"It was this morning, but my mom gave me a lift to get it after school. I came over here to check when I have practice again. We have the first game soon, and we've been practicing almost every hour. The coach has us check the schedule every day to see if we have to sneak in a morning practice, too."

It's cozy talking to Brad like this. Like I've slipped into a comfy easy chair.

"Would you like a ride home? You don't live too far do you?"

The cozy feeling goes away. He wants to give me a ride home. My heart thumps as if I've just finished running.

"I live about five miles from the school, east of Mill Valley. Will that take you out of your way?"

"No, that's fine. I live pretty close to there. Hop in, and I'll drive you home."

I pinch myself and feel the pain. This is not a dream. I've really been talking to Brad Morrow, and now I'm going to be getting a ride home with him. It dawns on my whole body what is happening, and my heart does cartwheels, while my breathing is so crazy I'm afraid to get up because I might faint. *Calm yourself; it's only a ride, not a date or anything. Breathe in and out, in and out, you have to get up and get into that car. You can't wait for the late bus when Brad offers you a ride.* I put my books away and stand. My erratic body starts to behave, and I get into Brad's car in front of the whole group of girls who come out of the school. They see me getting into Brad Morrow's car. This might be the best moment of my whole life. Wish I could press it forever like a rose. He starts the car, and I'm off on my first ride alone with a boy. Then it hits me. What will Jennifer think if she finds out? She will, of course, because Maura saw me drive off with Brad. I keep myself from looking back to see if she's on her phone.

I shove it all to the back of my mind and concentrate on how terrific it is to be sitting next to Brad Morrow and for the first time, not in a dream. I feel the cool leather seat and take in the wooden dashboard. I'm sitting in his brand new hunter green BMW convertible. Like the jeans I bought with Jennifer, which I still have to pay for, this is too good to be missed. I sit back and let out my breath.

Too scared to look at Brad, I concentrate on the scenery. The day has dressed up for me. Golden leaves hang on the trees, under them, and along the roadside. It's like the trees got a haircut, and it fell on the grass. Only most of it was blond, and it now looks like a blanket of yellow covering the ground. This depresses me. Even the trees have blond hair. Mine is still the same frizzy brown mess it's always been. Smoothing my hair with my hands, I peek over at Brad. His eyes are on the road, so I can look without his knowing. What does he see in me? I'm half tempted to ask him, but the words won't come into my mouth. But in a few minutes, I'm so happy I didn't say anything to him.

"So Carolyn, are you and Jennifer good friends?"

I wish I had a drink. My whole mouth feels like someone painted it with glue. My lips barely move to answer him.

"Sort of." I look over to check if he heard me. I'm afraid my lips won't be able to move if I have to speak again.

"It's just you're the only friend who came to see her in the nurse's office. I wonder why Maura didn't come. She and Jen have been friends since kindergarten. But you helped her the most today. When she came out of the fainting spell, she told me you took her to school this morning and brought her to the nurse."

I swallow, and there's a bitter taste in my mouth. Do I have a breath mint left in my pocket? Shoving my hand into the wide front pocket of my sweatshirt I search around. I grab something that feels like one and surreptitiously I check before I pop it into my mouth. I mean it could be anything, a button, a dime, an earring. Immediately it cools and freshens my mouth, and I'm able to answer Brad.

"Well...she...um...has been...um...really nice to me." Phew. I let out the breath I've been holding again.

"She can be great sometimes, but other times I don't know. She hardly pays attention to me. She's so concentrated on her gymnastics. You know how she wants to be in the Olympics. So she's always training and starving herself. Have you ever seen her eat anything but salad? I wonder how she stays alive. Even when we go out, all she'll order is salad. I guess she eats her meals at home. I know her coach watches the weight of all his people. It's worse than any sport, I'll tell you."

I nod my head. As Brad is talking, I notice he has a little dimple that appears and disappears near his full lips, and I want to take my hand and touch it. It takes all of my strength to keep my hand in my lap.

"So you're in Jen's math class? I guess you must be a math whiz, too. I'm awful in math. In fact, last year I practically didn't make the team because I almost flunked math. Good thing my teacher loved football and let me take the test over, or I'd be off the team this year. Now I've got a tutor so I'll pass this year. But he only comes once a week." He glances over at me and smiles. "In the meantime, I'm practically lost in math. This year's teacher doesn't care about football at all. So I'll really be screwed if I mess up again."

I smile back. He's even cuter when you get to know him. My cheeks are all warm, and I wonder how far it is to my house. I see a familiar street sign, and I know that we're close.

"You can turn right at the corner of Farmland Road and Wandering Springs Lane."

"Okay, where's your house?"

"Here it is, the next one on your right."

Brad turns into my driveway, and I see my dad is home already. I thank Brad for the ride and turn to leave the car. He stops me, touching my hand, which rests on the seat between us. I think my head might explode. I've never actually felt anything like this. It's like when you get an electric shock from walking on carpet when you touch someone.

"Thank you for helping Jennifer. I'm really glad she has you as a friend. Bye, Carolyn."

I'm numb and can't talk. I get out and stare as he leaves the driveway and turns onto Farmland Road.

I look down at the hand he touched. I hold it to my cheek palm side out and rub it gently back and forth on my face. I've got to tell someone, or I'm going to burst. I turn and run into the house, yell hi to Dad, and race upstairs to my room to call Becky or Janie, or both of them. I'll talk to whoever gets on the phone first. Now this is what I call an after school special.

Becky answers first, and I start babbling.

"Slow down, Carolyn, I can't understand a word you're saying."

"You'll never guess who just gave me a ride home."

"A ride home? Why were you at school so late? I swear you're living a double life these days. Are you a secret agent or something? Okay, let's see who could have given you a ride home? Um, Jennifer's mother?"

"No, but you're getting warm."

"Hmm, Maura?"

"No, now you're getting colder."

"Hmm, let's see. Jason Wadsworth the Third?"

"No, I don't even know him, silly."

"Okay, I give up, and this better be super good because I'll be in trouble if all my homework isn't finished before dinner. We're going somewhere tonight, and my mom wants me to enjoy myself and also get to bed on time."

"Who have I thought about for three years?"

"No, it can't be. It's him? Brad? You got a ride home with Brad Morrow? Jennifer's Brad? Does she know? Does anyone who knows her know?"

"Actually, Maura saw me get into his car. So it shouldn't be long before I get a call from Jennifer. If she has any strength to do that today."

"Geez, Carolyn, how did all of this happen? I want to know every little detail. Start from the beginning. How do you know him so well?"

Should I tell Becky about the day we ran into each other and how we both love pizza with pepperoni? How he kept my secret from Jennifer, and how he treated me when I saw her at the nurse's office? Should I tell her about what he said to me about how I was such a good friend to Jennifer? My head feels like a cement mixer with all of those sandbags emptied and churning in my brain. Too many lies, and now how can I keep anything more from my friend?

I swallow and begin.

"Well, I met Brad when Jennifer and I were doing the food survey."

"Shut up, you didn't!"

"Yeah, we met when he and I had the same favorite food. You know how I love pizza with pepperoni; well, that's his favorite, too. We both said it at almost the exact same time. It was freaky. Then she introduced us, and that's why he already knew me today at lunch."

I decide to leave out a lot of the story and figure I'll fill her in when I can tell the truth, whenever that happens.

"So I had to stay after today for one of my dumb classes, and when I was waiting for the late bus he came along and saw me. I was sort of sitting on the curb doing my homework, and he practically ran over me. Then he asked me if I wanted a ride. I swear that's what happened. There I was minding my business, waiting for the stupid late bus I hate. You know how I hate that bus. I think they go out of their way to let you off as far from your house as possible. So when he offered a ride, how could I refuse? I mean I thought I'd faint for sure because I totally lost my breath, and my face must have been purple or white or something. But he didn't seem to notice. Before I knew it, I was climbing into his car and settling into the soft leather seat in his amazing new BMW."

"Oh my God, Carolyn, I can't believe this. Did you think you were dreaming? I know I would have. How could this happen in real life? Go on. There's got to be more."

"So as I'm getting into the car, a group of girls who are basically all of Jennifer's friends, came out of school, and there was Maura. I know she saw me with Brad. I'm sure she'll tell Jennifer. So the most amazing experience of my life is going to turn out to be the worst one, too. Just my luck. I finally get a ride with my all-time crush, and it'll probably be my last day on earth. If I know Jennifer, she probably has a contract out on me now if Maura called her when she got home."

"I'm in shock, you know. What happened on the ride? What's he like in person? Is he as cute?"

"Oh, Becky, I'm floating. He thinks I'm a good friend to Jennifer, and he touched my hand. I don't think I can ever wash it again."

"Wow, so what did it feel like? This is a major first for you. First time in a car alone with a boy, and he touches your hand. But what will Jennifer do to you? Maura is so mean. Who knows what she'll say to Jennifer."

I hear a beep and realize there's another call coming through.

"Becky, I've got another call. Can I call you back? "

"Actually no, unless it's in two minutes. I've got to get my homework done before we go out tonight. But try anyway. I don't know if I can wait until tomorrow to find out if my best friend will still be alive." Becky laughs, and I press the flash button.

"Hello." I'm practically hyperventilating as I answer the phone.

"Carolyn, it's Jennifer. Just wanted to let you know how much I appreciate all you did for me today. Brad just called me and told me you came into the nurse's office after I passed out at lunch. You know you're the only person who cared enough about me to do that. My mom came for me, and when I got back home, Dad had sent me a bouquet of white roses. I wanted to throw those roses in the garbage. I'd rather he'd have been there instead. Sometimes I hate my dad."

Good, so far she hasn't said anything about the ride from Brad. I wonder if Maura didn't call yet to tell her. I keep my fingers crossed and decide to try my luck.

"Jennifer I'd really love to talk, but I have way too much homework to do. Did you get the math homework? Oh, by the way,

John in math said to say hi. He kept bugging me about you all period. I had to help him with his work. I wonder how he got into that class in the first place. Anyway, once he stopped pestering me about everything, he wasn't so bad. But he definitely missed you a lot."

"No, do you have it? I think every other teacher sent homework, but Mr. Armbruster wasn't there in his office, and I had to leave. So what is it?"

I give her the homework and find a way to get off the phone.

Breathing quickly in and out, in and out, I plop on my bed face up and close my eyes. It feels like this day has been as long as a week. Also I pray Jennifer won't find out about my ride with Brad. I'm starting to relax and beginning to dream one of my Brad and Carolyn dreams when the phone rings. I don't answer it. Let my answering machine take the message. Soon I hear a familiar voice, and it's more than angry. Damn she found out. What will happen to me now? This is so much worse than not breathing.

Chapter Seventeen

A few minutes later the phone rings again. I let it go for a while, but Dad picks it up and yells, "Carolyn, pick up your phone. There's someone for you. Are you home? I thought I heard you come in, but I wasn't sure. I must have been asleep when you got home."

"Did you find out who it is, Dad?" As if I needed to know, but I'm hoping it isn't who I think it is.

"No, but it's a girl. Pick it up. She's waiting for you."

I pick up the phone and tell myself I'm ready for this. I didn't do anything wrong. I just got a ride home. That's no big deal. Right?

"Hello?" It's Jennifer, as I thought.

"Carolyn, when we spoke earlier you left out something, didn't you?"

"I did?"

"I got a call from Maura a few seconds after we hung up, and she told me she saw you getting into Brad's car after school. Is this true?"

She knows already so I have to tell her the truth.

"He offered to give me a ride. I was waiting for the late bus when he saw me and asked if I needed a ride. Did I do something wrong?" I'm starting to get my breathing thing again, and I hope I'll be able to stay on the line.

"Well, Maura said he was looking at you like not in a friend way, if you know what I mean? And you were looking at him the same way."

"You're going to take Maura's word for something to do with me? She hates me, and you know it. How could she see what we looked like from where she was? She was coming out of school when I got into the car. She couldn't have seen our expressions." I take a deep breath and continue. "Anyway, Brad thinks I'm your friend, and he wanted to do something nice for one of your friends. Ask him. All he did was talk about you. He said I was the only person you knew who came to see how you were this afternoon. How is that possible?"

I hear a big sigh on Jennifer's side. "It's true, and I can't figure it out. Why didn't any of my friends come to see me today? It made me realize I've been a dope to think they care about me. When I really needed someone where were they?"

I actually find myself feeling sorry for her. What a day!

"What can I say? Maybe they were embarrassed by what happened and thought you might be, too. You know how most kids are. They just ignore everything and hope it'll go away. But I guess I'm not like most kids."

"No you're not, Carolyn. I'm beginning to realize that, and now I'm so sorry I treated you like I did. You know, it was always Maura who kept telling me it would be fun to pester you, and I went along with it. Since everyone always follows me, I guess it was pretty bad for you. But Maura and I have been friends since kindergarten, and she's always been on my side. I wonder why she didn't come to see me. I'm really hurt."

I can't believe Jennifer is defending Maura, and she wasn't even there when she needed her.

"Did you ask her when she called you?"

"Yeah, and she wouldn't give me a real answer. She said she had to go to class and couldn't be excused. But she's in our gym class."

I can't figure it out either, but I have my own problems, and I can't take on Jennifer's, too. I'm happy we're still talking.

"I think you and Maura need to have a real talk about this, but in the meantime, I have a lot of homework to do. So are you feeling any better?"

"I'm still a little weak but much better than this afternoon. My mom is making me this huge dinner tonight. She heard about my only eating salad at lunch, and now she's going to make sure I have three balanced meals."

Jennifer sounds like her mom is giving her a punishment.

"I have gymnastics practice in the morning, so I don't know what I'm going to do," she continues. "My coach said I couldn't gain any more weight."

Jennifer is still worried about gaining weight? If she thinks she's still too fat, what should I think about myself?

"Jennifer you are the perfect size. How much more weight can you lose?"

"I have to be at performance weight because we have a big meet coming up soon."

"What will you do? If you keep up what you're doing now, you're going to wind up in the hospital soon."

"I don't know. If I don't eat, I get weak and faint. But if I eat, I always worry I'll gain weight. So I have to get rid of my food. I can't tell my parents, or they'll go through the roof. And yet my dad, especially, gets me so mad I can't stand it."

Oh, no. Jennifer is going to tell me more about her problem. I tell myself to give some excuse and hang up, but really I'm fascinated by her thoughts. Who would guess Jennifer's life is so complicated? So I stay on the line, and she keeps talking.

"Then, even when I've told myself I'm going to stop, and believe me, I've tried a lot of times to stop, a thing he does or says to me will make me so angry I do it to spite him." Jennifer starts crying now, and I feel so lost. I wish I had hung up on her earlier. Now it's too late.

"Well, I think you should tell your mom about what you do. Do you think you could?"

"No, I can't tell either of them. They think I'm wonderful and popular, and I'm on my way to the Olympics. It's better for them not to know. I've kept it a secret this long, so why now?"

"How did you explain the lunchtime thing to them?"

"My mom thinks I have some kind of anemia. I may have to go to the doctor, and I'm not looking forward to that. In fact, she did make me an appointment for tomorrow. But I can't go. We have practice before and after school. The meet is next Saturday. If I do well in this one, I'll be able to go on to the county meet, and then the state meet, and finally the national one. That's the big one where they pick the people who will be on the Olympic Team. So this meet next Saturday is probably the most important day of my life."

"Jennifer, I've seen you in gym, and you are fantastic. You shouldn't worry. You'll do great."

"Right, but you're not a gymnast, so you don't see the little mistakes I make. But I'm working on them, and I hope to be ready for the meet. I can't think of anything else."

I have to get off the phone. I can't take this conversation anymore. Jennifer's life always gives me a headache.

"So are you still angry with me?" I remind her why she called. "I promise I'll ask you if he ever wants to give me a ride again." Why do I always sound like I'm the underling with Jennifer? Then I think of what she looks like and what her life is like and add in Brad. I'd still rather be like Jennifer than anyone I know, especially myself. This is so weird I have to get off the phone immediately.

"No, I guess I jumped to conclusions too quickly. It's not like I can't get any other guy I want. Right? I mean Brad is okay, and he's a really great guy. Didn't he stay with me today and everything? I just don't have enough time for him. I have to think of my gymnastics now. Concentrate on that and only that. So maybe you can spend a little time with him if he wants. It'll only be as friends, right?" Jennifer says.

"You're not mad at me; I'm so glad." I let out the breath I've been holding while she gave her answer. "Okay, I'll let you know if he ever wants to see me again for any reason. By the way, where is your meet being held?"

"It's in the school gym this time, and there'll be five teams who all compete at once. You can come. In fact, I want you to come. I consider you my friend now."

Wow. Despite all the horrible things she has done to me and said about me, this is amazing and very unexpected. I wonder if it is real or just another bribe in case she needs me again. In spite of it all, I get a warm glow, and I find myself smiling.

"Great. I have to go now. See you in school. Eat your mom's food and try to control yourself. You haven't eaten anything in a while so it can't put any weight on you," I say.

"Okay, I'll think about what you said. See you tomorrow in math. Bye."

"Bye, Jennifer." I hang up the phone and lay back on my bed thinking.

Jennifer and I are friends. How did this happen? She's going to let me be friends with Brad. Will Becky and Janie still talk to me when they find out about my being Jennifer's friend now? It's amazing how events can move so quickly. But my problems aren't over. I still have to tell my friends the truth about everything. Neither of them knows I'm trying out for cheerleaders tomorrow. Yikes, I have to practice.

I bound off my bed and start the cheers, practicing until Dad yells up to me, "What's going on Carolyn? I feel like there's an elephant walking in your room."

"Nothing Dad, I'm just practicing," I say, a little out of breath as I come to the head of the stairs.

"Practicing what?"

I decide to tell him and empty one of my sandbags. It's such a relief.

"Dad, I'm trying out for the cheerleading squad tomorrow," I tell him, sitting on the sofa opposite his chair. "That's why I was late today. They had us sign up, and they taught us the cheer we'll be doing for the tryouts." I look into his eyes, and he looks puzzled.

"Cheerleading? I didn't know you were interested. Well, you should do great. You were always good in dance. I wonder why you stopped going to your lessons. We never understood it. All of a sudden in sixth grade you decided to stop."

I remember the day I knew I couldn't go back to dance school again. I had on this form fitting leotard and tights showing my whole misshapen body, but I loved dance and didn't care what I looked like. I forgot all about it when I was dancing. But a few of the girls, and come to think of it one of them was Maura, made fun of me so much in the locker room, I felt uncomfortable going into the dance studio. But I went in, and when we were doing some group dances for the teacher at the end of the class, one girl, maybe Maura, yelled out, "Here comes the hippo."

I had to continue with my group and afterwards I ran out of the room. I loved the class, but after that day, I couldn't go to dance. It's one thing to think you're a hippo, but it's another to hear it from someone's mouth. I remember how it was hard to breathe, and I sat on the bench feeling light-headed. No one spoke to me except Becky, who came and put her arms around me. I couldn't tell either Mom or Dad why I wouldn't go back, but they let me quit. I couldn't tell them why after all this time.

"Do you want to know a secret, Dad? I've been practicing the cheers for a whole year. Becky and Janie and I used to go to the games last year, and I learned them. So I found a pair of pom-poms one day at the football game and brought them home. Can I show you one of the cheers, and you'll tell me what you think?"

"Sure, you know I always love to see you perform," Dad says.

I get this big burst of energy and give Dad a huge hug. I wish Mom was here, too, but I'll finally have an audience even if it is only one person.

Running upstairs to grab my pom-poms, I feel like I'm ten pounds lighter. I glide back down. One secret's out, and it's good to empty one sandbag. Max seems to have caught my excitement, and he runs around in circles while I demonstrate my cheering for Dad. Now all I need is to make the cheerleading squad.

Chapter Eighteen

It's finally the end of school and time for cheerleading tryouts. The gym is buzzing with girls practicing everything from cartwheels to jumps and twirls.

"We're starting in five minutes. If your name isn't on the list, you won't be allowed to try out."

The other girl continues speaking to us. "All of you have to leave the gym and wait outside. You will have three minutes to perform by yourself. You must present the cheer you learned yesterday and another one you have chosen. Let's begin."

I join the girls who walk outside, since my number is close to twenty. I practice my cheer, but now I'm having second thoughts. What a stupid idea to think I, Carolyn Samuels, who spent all last year as Jennifer Taylor's punching bag, could be a cheerleader. I'll leave now and not bother to try out. No one will miss me.

Once the decision is made, it's easy to move toward the exit and inch away from the crowd. It should be even easier to walk out of the front door, wait for the bus, and go home, still a loser and no closer to my goal. But I'm stopped at the last minute when I see Brad coming down the hall. He's got a spring in his step. My breathing does the usual skip, and I can't move. I try the breathe in and breathe out plan, but my body isn't cooperating. I start to feel faint like what happened in gym. Mortified in case I'll faint in front of Brad, I collapse against the wall and sit with my hands around my knees. Maybe it'll pass, and I'll be able to go home. I try to make myself as invisible as possible, but it's too late. Brad sees me and waves. My heart flip-flops, and I know if I weren't already on the floor, I'd have fallen at that moment.

He comes toward me, and I start panting like a dog. This is awful, and I have to pull myself together before he gets here. He'll ask me about the tryouts. I can't leave now. I force myself to stand, and I start practicing my cheer. I've been practicing this one in secret for over a year in front of the mirror. I know it cold. I'm at the part where I jump into the air and yell Yay when Brad reaches me.

"Hey, Caroline, nice jump." He grins, and I'm glad I stayed. Brad Morrow talking to me and grinning causes a traffic jam in the little space left to pass in the hallway as the other girls pass by and rubberneck like I'm an accident on the highway.

"Hi, Brad," I say hoping my heart won't beat out of my body. Could that happen I wonder? "Thank you. Did you really think it was good? I'm so nervous about trying out today." My breath is coming in spurts, and I feel like I've run around the track for a mile. I'm not sure I can keep breathing. Breathe, Carolyn, breathe. I use the hated words to keep me focused.

"If you do it like you just did it now, you're sure to get onto the squad. You're great."

My heart leaps up to my throat, and I feel a smile spilling from my mouth. Brad likes the way I did the cheer. He didn't laugh, and he didn't say I looked like a geek or a wounded hippo like I feel.

"Couldn't see any difference between what I see on the field and what you did. If I were the judge, I'd let you on the team." He smiles and leans against the wall with his shoulder. I want to go over to him and hug him, but I don't.

I lean my back against the opposite wall and face him. Between my breathing problem and my heart beating like a bongo drum, I have to lean against something, or I'll collapse in a heap at his feet

"Do you have long to wait before your tryout?" Brad says.

"I'm number nineteen, and there's twenty of us here. Doesn't seem like that many, does it?"

A mischievous gleam comes into his eyes as he looks at me. "You know I just realized I'm the only boy here. There's twenty girls in short skirts and skimpy tops and me. That's going to be a long wait, but I think I'll manage." He grins again.

"You don't have to wait for me." I feel like I might explode. All this tension about the tryout, and now Brad wanting to wait for me.

"You would? Well, I was going to take the late bus. Don't you have football practice or something?"

"No game this weekend. We practiced a little this afternoon. But maybe you don't want me to wait. I'll go. See you on Monday." You know, I'd like to wait with you. Do you need a ride?

"No, I mean if you want to wait, it's okay with me. You know I hate the late bus. Thank you." Right, I told Brad it was just okay when I'm so happy I could do cartwheels down the hallway. I try to remember every detail and press them into my brain. Brad is wearing a Mill Valley High School Varsity T-shirt in purple with gold letters, our school colors. He's carrying his jacket in his right hand, and he's slung it over one shoulder. But it's his smile that gets me all melty. I'd be happy just looking at Brad's face all day.

But I promised I'd let Jennifer know if I did anything with Brad again. So I know I have to do the right thing now.

"Brad, I have to make a phone call."

I open my cell phone and dial Jennifer. I have it only for emergencies, but I consider this an emergency.

"Hi, Carolyn. So what's up?" Jennifer answers after a couple of rings.

"Hi Jennifer, remember when you told me to tell you if Brad ever gave me a ride again?"

"Yeah, that was yesterday. I do have a memory." The old Jennifer comes roaring back.

"Well, he's here at school and wants to give me another ride home today. Do you mind?"

Silence on the other end, and I start feeling like I did the wrong thing.

"No, go ahead. You guys are really getting friendly, huh?"

"I guess so. It's more like he seems to pop up in the same places I am. I didn't ask him. He suggested it. Thanks, Jennifer. I'll tell you all about it when I get home."

"Sure, Carolyn, and you can call me Jen."

No way. I can call her Jen. I can't speak anymore and mumble, "Bye," and hang up.

This is so spectacular I feel like the halls are going to fill with singers and dancers shouting to everyone, "Carolyn can call her Jen." I want to run back and tell all the girls who are trying out for the cheerleading team I can call Jennifer, Jen. Wonder what I'll have to do to pay for this ride with Brad. I'm willing to do her homework for a week if I can be alone with Brad. For the thousandth time, I wonder if Jennifer really likes Brad. Now we're friendly, I don't want to do anything to spoil our friendship, so it's hard to go back and be with Brad. But at least I don't have to feel guilty anymore. My breathing comes back to normal, and I practically glide back to where Brad is standing looking like he's just scored a touchdown. He smiles at me as I walk toward him. Maura glares at me across the corridor.

I ignore Maura's evil eye and move next to Brad.

"Brad, you know Jennifer and I are friends now.

"Yeah, I know. She thinks you're great and told me to come over and kind of be there for you in case you needed someone."

"I just called her, and she didn't say anything about that. Were you supposed to keep it secret?"

Brad looks at me with his eyes all squinty and smiles. He looks like Max when I catch him trying to eat food off the counter. "Secret? No, I don't think so. Jen kind of asked me to stop by and check if you needed a ride." Wow, Jennifer has so many sides to her. She is thinking about me and sent Brad. I feel like soap scum for thinking about him as a possible boyfriend.

I wait for my turn and practice a few of my steps while I wait.

"Number nineteen," the leader calls, and I rush over to the gym door.

"Give us the cheer we taught to you," the head cheerleader says when I get through the door.

As I perform the cheer we've been taught, the one I've been practicing for over a year in front of my mirror, I'm mentally crossing my fingers and praying at the same time I will get through this without falling or disgracing myself.

"Okay, let's see the cheer you picked." I glance outside and see Brad peering in through the narrow windows in the gym door. I take a deep breath and force myself to concentrate on my cheer.

"Does it matter if my choice is the same one you taught to us? I've been practicing it all year."

"It isn't usual," the head cheerleader says, "but if you feel comfortable, we'll allow you to repeat the cheer we taught to you. "

My feet do the steps, and my mouth says the words, but it doesn't feel real. My thoughts repeat, don't fall, don't fall, don't fall. until the rhythm mixes with the chanting, and the movement continues automatically.

"Stop, your time is up," the head cheerleader says. I blew it, judging from the expression on their faces. I'll never be a cheerleader. It was a dumb plan.

"When will we know how we did?" I ask. The girl gives me a look, which tells me I'm not the first to ask that question. Uh, oh, does this part count, too, I wonder? If I get the head cheerleader angry at me, will it ruin my chances? My breathing does its thing, and I hope I'll be able to get out of the gym without fainting. With Brad's face in front of me, I start toward the door.

"Carolyn Samuels, that's your name, right?"

For a second I'm blank. Then I answer, "Yes, did you want me to stay here?"

"No, but the answer to your question is we'll let you know. We'll post the list tomorrow morning. But everyone who is picked will get a phone call by tomorrow night."

Number twenty, Maura, gives me an evil look as we pass each other at the doorway. Suddenly I'm overcome with fear and can barely keep breathing.

"Are you finished now, Carolyn?"

I turn to Brad and smile at him. He waited all this time to give me a ride. I realize how stupid I was to think I could ever have him. He's only here because Jennifer sent him. Anyway, I'm alone with Brad, and that's all that counts.

Chapter Nineteen

The ride home with Brad is a blur to me, but I feel like a princess getting out of her carriage when Brad opens the car door for me. He gives me his hand, and I place mine in his, and my dream is complete. As I step onto my driveway and feel the familiar ruts and hills of its texture on my sneakered foot, I realize this is true.

"Thank you for bringing me home again. Jennifer is lucky to have you."

"My pleasure. This isn't exactly a hardship for me, you know. I like hanging out with you, and since I wasn't doing anything much, I thought I'd give you a ride. Anytime you need another one, just holler. That is if I don't have practice or anything."

"Sure you won't mind my tagging along with you and Jennifer?"

"Of course not, you're Jennifer's friend, and if it's okay with her, then it's fine."

"I've gotta go in and start my homework. Thanks again. It really helped having you there when I tried out. Now I have to sweat it all night. I'll be surprised if I get a minute of sleep."

"Well, from what I saw, you have no problems. I didn't see anyone who did those cheers better than you."

My face feels like a furnace, and I'm sure it's beet red up to my ears. So I duck out of there and shout to Brad from the safety of my front door.

"Bye, and I hope you're right." I wave as he turns out of my driveway, and he puts up his hand to show he's seen it.

I run into my house. Dad is sitting in his usual spot reading the newspaper and watching the international news. It's times like these I wish Mom were home. If she were here, we'd probably discuss this problem, which keeps getting worse and worse. Over steaming cups of cocoa, she'd listen to me. What should I do? Is it right to let your friend's boyfriend take you home twice without her there in the car? I make myself a cup of sugar free cocoa and walk into the living room. Dad looks up and gives me a big smile.

"Hey, didn't see you come in. I guess I had my attention on the news."

"That's okay, Dad, I didn't want to disturb you."

"So, what's happening? How were the tryouts? Will you hear soon?"

"Tomorrow, they're posting a list. Can you drive me up there to see it? I mean they did say they'd call too, but I'd like to know as soon as possible."

"Sure, honey. Get me up in the morning, and maybe we'll have breakfast together."

"Great, Dad. You know I really miss Mom. When are her hours going to change? I love being with you, but it's different with Mom."

"Honey, she said this is the final day of her late hours, she'll be home at the usual time starting next week."

My heart gives a leap of joy. I mean I'm old enough to be without my mommy, but I didn't realize how much I missed the talks we used to have before bedtime. I guess that's when I felt most comfortable, and she'd sit on my bed, and I'd open up and tell her the things that had been bothering me all day. Wish she were home tonight so I can figure out what is going on with Brad and me. Can't wait until tomorrow to see if I made the cheerleading team.

* * * *

"Hi Carolyn, here to see if you made the team? " Jennifer says to me next day at school. I'm wondering what she's doing there on a Saturday.

Maura comes walking up to Jennifer and me. I guess Jennifer came with her.

"Hey, Jen, let's go inside. Can't wait to see if I made the team. I know my cheerleading was great. Of course I made it. But let's check anyway."

I hear Maura's smug voice, and I want to hide. I've gotten sort of comfortable with Jennifer, but somehow when Maura's there, she kind of ignores me. I hate to revert back to my invisible state again. So I walk beside Jennifer, and Maura sees me next to her. She gets her smelling pickles look and grabs Jennifer's arm to move away…Jennifer stays put and turns to me.

"Carolyn, let's go inside and check, okay?" She grabs my arm and stares back at Maura.

Maura strides through the door alone, and it practically slams in our faces. Wonder why Jennifer stayed with me? We both go through the front door to the list posted on the bulletin board next to the gym.

There's a huge crowd around the list, and if I weren't with Jennifer, I'd have to wait until everyone in front of me checked it. But being with Jennifer has its perks, and the crowd divides to let us through. As we get closer to the list, I start to have breathing problems. What if I'm not on it? What if Maura made the team, and I didn't? Maybe Brad was lying, and I was awful yesterday. He just didn't want to hurt my feelings.

I force myself to breathe in and out and finally we reach the list. I hold my breath and probably I'm turning blue, but I'm so worried about seeing the list. I keep my eyes shut and only open them when I hear this big shout from Jennifer.

"Carolyn, come look. Don't you want to see for yourself? You're on the list. There you are and so is Maura. How great is that? Both of my friends are going to be together." She shouts to Maura to come over and take a look. Like melting ice cream, Maura's face changes. The meanness dissolves, and I see an actual smile on her lips. Then she's laughing and hugging Jennifer. Jennifer turns to me and hugs me. Soon everyone is crowding around, and I find out two more girls were picked. I'm so excited I can barely walk. But it doesn't matter, because I don't care. Jennifer helped me, and I'm where I've always dreamed I'd be. Who would have thought I'd be a cheerleader? I wonder if maybe the head cheerleaders need glasses. Did they really see me? Or maybe I'm not as bad looking as I've always thought.

As I rush out to tell Dad I made the team, all these kids stop me and say congratulations, like I'm a star. Jennifer walks along with me, and she's overjoyed.

"Geez, I feel like I had a little part in this, you know."

"Yes, thank you, Jennifer, for everything you've done for me."

"Why so formal? I mean we know each other well enough for you to call me Jen."

"I know, but it's so hard for me. Let me get used to everything first, okay?"

We've reached the car, and Dad gives me a big smile when he sees my expression. I say goodbye to Jennifer, and she moves over to Maura and starts talking. But as we leave the school, Jennifer waves to me. I wave back at her.

When we get home, Mom says someone named Tammy called to tell me I was on the cheerleading team. Mom has this huge smile on her face, and she hugs me, too.

"I'm so proud of you, and I'm sorry I couldn't be there to help you when you were trying out. Dad said you knew the cheers and looked great. I knew you'd get there."

Before I can stop them, my eyes are wet, and I want to crawl into my mom's arms and cuddle with her like when I was a little kid.

I choke out a few words. "Mom...I...have...so much..." Then my brain takes over, and I realize what I'm about to say can't happen. Mom won't understand why I didn't tell her immediately. Then I'll have to explain how I did Jennifer's homework, and how I've lied to Becky and Janie, and the last and most painful part. How I got friendly with Jennifer so she could help me get popular. But how am

I repaying her? I'm hanging out with her boyfriend. Jennifer and Maura were right to look at me the way they did. I am toe jam.

"Carolyn, are you okay? You look kind of strange."

"I've just got a lot on my mind and tons of homework to do. If it's okay with you, I'll go up and start it now. I love you, Mom." Inside me a hard shell is cracking, and I'm amazed I don't look like those windshields that crackle when they're hit by a rock. It takes all my effort to climb the stairs, and I collapse on my bed staring at my magazine photos on the wall.

Chapter Twenty

A ringing jolts me awake. I must have dozed off, because it's three hours later. The remnants of a dream haunt me as I reach for the phone. In my dream, I'm a gymnast and walking on a balance beam. It's a big competition, and I've almost finished. My feet are steady, inching along the distance between the two ends of the beam. I'm almost to the end, and the audience is so silent you can hear the sound of my slipper-clad feet bouncing on the beam. For my dismount, I perform a perfect triple somersault and land on my feet with my arms up in the traditional exit gesture. I turn to leave, acknowledging the applause of the audience. It's all so perfect except at the last minute, I trip over a mat and land flat on my face. The fickle audience turns on me and laughs. Then suddenly I'm in my cheerleading outfit at the first game of the season. We all run onto the field and start our cheer. I'm cheering along with a big smile on my face and jump into the air. At that moment, I hear the sound of ripping material, and when I land, the audience is laughing. I turn to look, and there it is a huge rip right down the back of my outfit. I run off the field, too embarrassed to continue.

I wake up almost unable to breathe and blink a few times to assure myself I'm in my bed and not on a muddy football field. What was that dream all about? I'm not a gymnast. I've learned to do a few somersaults and cartwheels, but I'm not great. It's all too weird. So I decide to forget about it and remember all of my homework. My feet are hitting the floor when the phone rings.

"Carolyn, you'll never guess what happened?" Jennifer sounds out of breath on the other end.

"Jennifer, are you okay? You sound like you're having a breathing attack."

"Yeah, I just heard this amazing news. You know how I told you the meet next weekend is going to be the one where they choose the Olympic finalists? Well, my coach just told me I have a great chance of making it to the finals. He wants me to work with him every day this week before school."

"So what's your problem? I thought this is what you want."

"It is, and I can barely speak I'm so excited. It's just that I will have to go home right after school and do my homework. I won't have any time to go out or anything. The meet's on Saturday."

"That's okay, you've been working for this for years. You should go for it."

"I know, but what about Brad? I won't be able to see him at all this week. I can't even go to the football game on Friday night. I promised him I'd be there. What am I going to do?"

Jennifer whines on, but I don't hear she's that upset. It's more like she has to give up something, and Brad is a front row center ticket for a great rock concert.

"Jennifer, take a breath, and I'll help you figure out something to tell Brad. Aren't you going to the Homecoming dance with him?" I remind her of what she told me yesterday.

"I'm counting on it, but I don't have a dress to wear. Do you want to go shopping with me? I always like to have someone else's opinion, and since Maura is barely talking to me now, it's got to be you."

In typical Jennifer fashion, she's managed to make me feel good and bad at the same time. Being with her is like being near one of those air coolers in a broiling hot room. The heat comes on and blasts you with its warmth. But you're right by the window, and the vents of the air cooler blow cold air until you shiver. I never really know where I stand with her. I miss Becky and Janie, but I don't think I can invite them along with us.

"I wish I had a way to do my homework and still see Brad." There's a pause, then Jennifer continues. "Do you remember the first day of school when you fainted and begged me to cover it up for you?"

"Of course I remember. That was a traumatic experience for me. I would have done anything to keep that from getting out. I was petrified, but I begged you anyway."

"I saw your pathetic look and figured I'd use you to get my homework done. When you agreed, I couldn't believe it. You saved my life that night. We got back from that stupid dinner at ten, and I was wiped."

I wonder why she remembered this now. Then I know why. Jennifer is like a snake lying hidden until it needs to strike.

"Well," she hesitates, "if you would do my math homework, which takes me the longest, I'll be able to do the rest. It'll save me tons of time, and I can see Brad after school."

Honey drips from her voice, and I figure why not?

Chapter Twenty-One

On Monday, Jennifer and I do the same switch we did the second day of school before we head into math class. This time we walk in together, and I notice John can't decide who he should look at when we enter. It's a strange feeling for me to know a guy is looking at me as if I deserved it. So I keep my eyes down and ease into my seat.

"Hi, you gorgeous twosome." Me a part of a gorgeous twosome? Maybe John needs glasses, too.

Jennifer turns and gives him her usual dazzling smile. John looks as if he is about to light up and fly around the room. I really think he rises from his seat a little when I see him.

Mr. Armbruster drones on about some assignment we need to do in three weeks. I try to concentrate, but my mind is hearing gibberish.

"Did you girls catch that assignment?" John looks around at the rest of the class.

"No, I wasn't paying attention. Anyway we have three weeks to find out what it is," I say. Somehow today I can't get all worked up about school. Too much else on my mind.

The loudspeaker comes on and announces practice for all cheerleaders after school and reminds the football team there is an early practice to get ready for the big Homecoming Game next Saturday. Also, there's an announcement about tickets being sold for the Homecoming Dance starting today at lunch.

"Jennifer, how did your gymnastic practice go?" I stage whisper across the aisle to her.

She whispers back, "Great. My coach says I might win on Saturday."

I guess we would have continued like this, but Mr. Armbruster looks over at us and gives us his 'are you paying attention?' look. Jennifer and I try to figure out what has been going on in class. Lucky for us John decided he should pay attention, so we both copy what he's got in his book. But I can't concentrate on this class at all, and I'm so thankful when the bell rings and class is over.

When the morning ends, I've never been so happy to have lunch. But I'm not hungry. What's wrong with me? Maybe it's the first cheerleading practice that is causing my stomach to knot. I get my usual lunch and stare at it with disinterest. I can't seem to get my spoon to my mouth. Am I sick of yogurt? But it wouldn't matter what food was sitting in front of me.

Becky, Janie, and I are still at Jennifer's table. I look up and meet Brad's eyes. Everyone else is eating their lunch and doesn't look up. Brad is smiling at me, and I realize he's about to speak.

"Are you spending too much time with Jennifer, Carolyn? You haven't touched your lunch, and I know this isn't normal for you."

I smile back. On Sunday, I told Becky and Janie about making the cheerleading team, so I don't have to hide the next words.

"I guess I'm kind of nervous about the first cheerleading practice. I mean what if I goof up on the cheer, and then everyone messes up because of me? Or what if I start cheering, and my uniform rips?"

Brad looks at me as if I'm a small child on his knee.

"Carolyn, how do you think up these ridiculous things? You'll be great. I told you that when you tried out. They knew it and picked you. What else do you need? You think way too much."

He peeks over at Jennifer who is picking at her salad. "I always wonder why you bother to get anything for lunch. Every day you get a salad and move your fork through it. But it never quite gets to your mouth." Jennifer looks up at Brad with the look I saw too much of last year. "Sometimes it looks like it might reach your mouth, but then you put it down." I wonder why Brad doesn't stop now.

Jennifer glares at him and starts eating furiously. She attacks her salad with her fork and stuffs in so much green it takes her forever to talk. But she does.

"Brad, I hate salad. I hate the feel of the lettuce in my mouth. But I have to stay at this weight for my gymnastic meet." Jennifer's voice sounds louder and angrier as she continues. "So bug off and don't bother me about food, okay? I have enough on my mind this week as it is. If I have to think about food, too, I'll lose it for sure."

Jennifer looks over at me for assurance. I nod my head, and she motions for me to say something, too.

"Um, yeah, she has too much on her mind this week. Bug her next week, okay?"

I see gratitude in Jennifer's eyes for my support. I want to tell Brad all about Jennifer's problem, but it isn't the time, and she'd probably tear me apart if I said anything.

Brad looks from one to the other of us with a question in his eyes.

"Are you two working together now? I mean all I asked is why did you get lunch if you were only going to pick at it?"

Jennifer's eyes soften. The Scarlet O'Hara look comes back on her face. Maybe she realizes she has gone too far this time.

"I'm sorry, Brad. I didn't mean to snap at you, but I'm totally stressed. Maybe we can hang out after school today. Can you?" Jennifer lowers her lashes, and I see Brad give in to her act. You'd think he'd realize she can turn this on or off whenever she wants, but he doesn't seem to care.

Brad's face looks like a spotlight has lit him from inside. He puts his arm around Jennifer, and I get this sinking feeling deep inside my body. No matter what happens, Brad will always be with Jennifer. The stupid scenes I've constructed crumble, and I feel tears begin.

"Hey, I've got to get going," I say because I know I'm going to break down in tears any second. Janie's at lunch with us, because her gym teacher left, and they're having the two classes together. Becky and Janie get up with me, and we all go into the bathroom nearest the lunchroom.

Safely inside the bathroom, we all get into a stall together. I let my eyes do what they want, and soon I'm totally sobbing. Becky puts her arms around me and tries to comfort me.

"What's going on? I thought you were thrilled to be a cheerleader, and you're sitting at Jennifer's table."

"Becky, everything's gotten so complicated." I have to tell her and Janie about my feelings for Brad, or I'll explode.

"Okay, we have a few minutes between now and gym, spill it."

I see the concern in her friendly blue eyes, and I feel like I'm up on the platform for the zip line, and I have to step down. I start to breathe funny, and Janie pats me on the back.

"Squeeze in tight, and if anyone comes in, forget it." I grab my friends close to me.

"Whatever you want Carolyn. You know we're both here for you." Becky and Janie say together, and we join hands and form a tight circle.

I take the step, and open my mouth to tell them. "There's so much I want to tell you guys, but you deserve to hear it all. Can you trust me for a little longer? I promise you won't be sorry. Meanwhile, you guys are the best. Thanks for being here when I needed you."

We all hug each other, and I dry my eyes just as the bell rings, and the bathroom door opens for Jennifer.

"Carolyn, are you okay? You left in such a hurry." I open the stall door and see the concern in her eyes.

"Sure, Jen." Becky and Janie glance back at me with a question in their eyes and leave the bathroom without me. I guess they're angry I didn't tell them anything. Can't wait to tell the whole story to my best friends. "See you in gym," I shout to Jennifer as I leave the bathroom and hurry to catch up with Becky and Janie.

* * * *

At cheerleading practice, I realize I fit right into the team, and I'm so surprised. I concentrate on my steps and learn the new ones. The rest of the week flies by, and soon it's Friday, and Jennifer and I are talking in the hallway at the end of the day.

"So are you a little nervous about tomorrow?

"Sure who wouldn't be? I mean I've been training for this all my life. But my coach says I have a really good chance to make it to the county finals if I do well tomorrow. He's going to train the top three from each meet. We'll have one more later. You know I haven't really eaten anything all week. Do you want to come over tonight?"

"No, but thanks anyway. I've promised to spend the night with Becky and Janie. We haven't spent a Friday night together in a while, and we need to catch up, you know?"

"Well, it's pizza night tonight, and I know how much you love pizza with pepperoni, you and Brad. I thought we'd just hang out, and maybe your being there might help me feel less nervous. You know maybe keep me from doing my thing."

I know what her thing is. She means if I come over, then maybe I'll keep her from eating too much and getting rid of it. I don't see how I can. Did my being there help the last time? Anyway, I promised Becky and Janie we'd do our Friday night stuff.

"It's tempting, but I'll have to take a rain check. Why don't we do it next Friday night?"

"Okay, we'll see. We'd better hurry, or Ms. Gaylon is going to mark us late if we don't get moving."

We run to gym, get into our gym clothes quickly, and make it just as the bell rings. Janie sits next to Becky, then me, and Jennifer

163

sits on my other side. Becky gives her a quick smile, which doesn't reach her eyes, when we line up. Was it only a month ago I was scared of Jennifer? I'm feeling pretty good when Maura looks over at me with daggers in her eyes. What's with her anyway?

Gym moves along with no special problems, and aside from Maura's permanent frost for me, I'm feeling pretty good. I'm looking forward to being with my old friends and having our familiar Friday night.

"Carolyn, are you coming on the bus today? I'll save you a seat," Becky asks me as she gets to the exit door of the girl's lockers.

"That'd be great, and I can't wait for tonight. You and Janie are coming over around seven, right?"

I've decided to have them over at my house, and Mom is getting ready by stocking up on all of our favorites. She's feeling guilty about all the time I had to spend without her, so she's even baking something for us.

When I get home, there are freshly baked chocolate chocolate chip cookies, my favorite, and I grab one. As I'm biting into the hot, gooey cookie, the phone rings.

"I'll get it, Mom." I rush to answer it.

"Hi, Carolyn. Just thought I'd call and see what you're doing. I'm going crazy here."

"Aren't you with Brad now?"

"He had to do something for his mother this afternoon and can't see me until tonight. So, I'm wondering. I have a few hours before he comes over, and we didn't get to the mall yet for my dress for the dance. Mom says she'll take me. Do you want me to pick you up? I have to be home by seven for Brad anyway."

I figure it'll only be a few hours, and I have nothing special to do until they come over, so I ask Mom if it's okay if I leave for a few hours. I get a few dollars from her, too. She's got a little more spending money since she did this special project.

We get to the mall before I know it, and soon we're looking through racks of dresses that look like they're perfect for the dance.

"How about this one?" I show Jennifer a dress made of a crinkly, shiny material in pink with thin straps.

"I like this one." She holds up a very tight black dress with a low cut front. Then she grabs a couple of others, and we go back to try them on.

Jennifer looks so good in all of these it's hard to make a choice. She looks at herself in the mirror, turning, twisting and adjusting each dress until she is satisfied. But not one dress is her favorite.

In another store, she finds the one she wants. It's a simple silk and organza strapless top with layers of material for the skirt swirled around so the bottom looks like a rose. I've never seen anything quite like it before, and when she gets to the cashier, and I see the price, I understand why. I can never afford to live like Jennifer Taylor. Her life is so different from mine it's scary. I would love to be able to spend hundreds of dollars on a dress for a dance. I won't be going to the Homecoming Dance. No one has asked me.

"Carolyn, why don't you try on one of those dresses? Do you have anything at all to wear to the dance if someone does ask you this week?"

I figure why not and start trying on some of the dresses I have been drooling over. I start with my old size, but those are too big, and I'm thrilled. I've gone down a whole size. Wow. Why don't I feel good about how I look?

"Try on this one." Jennifer hands me a pale blue silk dress with only a sheer fabric covering it. It's got little straps and a draped scooped neckline.

"Okay, and maybe I'll take a few of these other ones in a smaller size." I know it's playacting, but I'm having so much fun.

Standing in front of the mirror, I don't believe it's me. Where are all the bulges and my hippo hips? The dress covers all of this, and I bathe in the mirror's gentle image. Wow, wonder what Brad would think if he saw me now?

"Carolyn, don't bother trying on any of the other dresses. This is the one you have to have. What's the price?"

I glance at the price tag and gag. It's way over two hundred dollars. Cinderella has to go back to her rags. No dress for me.

But Jennifer won't let me leave the dress. "Do you have a layaway plan here?" she asks the cashier.

"Jennifer, Mom will kill me if I spend this much money on a dress. Do you know how long it will take me to pay for this?"

"I'll tell you what. How about if I pay you for doing my homework this week? If I pay you twenty dollars for every night, that's one hundred dollars. Then you might be able to get the rest off of your mom. How do you like that idea?"

Well, if it's business, then it might be okay. I nod my head in agreement, and a salesperson brings it to the cashier where she puts my name on it. I give them the money plus the extra Mom gave me, and I've got the dress.

"Oh, Carolyn, maybe I'll try to get you a date with someone for the Homecoming Dance. You've got to come in that dress. Won't everyone be surprised?"

All I can think of is Brad and how wonderful it would be to be wearing that pale blue dress at the same dance with him. At the same time, I feel really guilty. He belongs to Jennifer. Why can't my mind allow me to accept this? *You're evil Carolyn. Find another guy. Brad's taken.*

"Do you think you can?" Then I realize who she can get for my date for the dance. "Does Jason Wadsworth the Third have a date yet? You did say you were going to fix me up with him, and we'd all go out together."

"Yeah, I'll see what I can do. I'll ask Brad tonight, and I'll have Jason call you, okay?" Jennifer glances at her watch and decides to leave the store. "Look at the time. We'd better get going. You know this was fun, Carolyn." Jennifer's gratitude makes me feel even worse.

I get home in plenty of time to get ready for the night; and when the bell rings, I know I'm more than ready to let Becky and Janie know the truth, finally, about my double life.

Chapter Twenty-Two

We're all sprawled on my bed watching our favorite Friday night shows. Mom's snacks were so good we've practically eaten the plates. All that's left is a few chocolate chocolate chip cookies we're munching on now.

"You know we could close our eyes, and we'd be back to last year. Don't you feel that way?" I say. I feel a peacefulness I haven't felt all year tonight.

"Sure Carolyn, only it's not last year, and we're not all the same are we?" Janie says. She has a point, and I know I have to tell them now.

"You're right, you know. We aren't the same. I guess I've changed, and I haven't spent as much time with you guys as I used to. I have something to tell you, and I hope we'll still be friends afterward." I'm starting to have breathing problems and wonder if I'll be able to get through this without fainting.

"What do you have to tell us that's making you look like you're going to faint?" Becky focuses her attention on me.

"You have to promise me you'll stay the rest of the night when you hear this, okay?" They nod their heads and promise, so I continue.

I tell them everything that's happened between Jennifer and myself, and then I tell them about Brad and how we've become so friendly. While I'm talking, Becky and Janie have this look like they're about to be road kill. They open their eyes and mouths wide and stare at me. As each new revelation is heard, they gasp, and soon I see their expressions turning.

"You did her homework for money?" Becky says and puts her hands over her mouth.

"Well, I didn't realize it was going to be for money. She offered it to me so I could get the dress. You have to see this dress on me. It looks so amazing."

"You're trying to break up Jennifer and Brad?" Janie says, and her voice goes up at the end. "But you can't break up Jennifer and Brad just because you have a crush on him."

Janie is right, and I know she is. I don't really want to break them up or hurt Jennifer. She's been more than nice to me.

Becky and Janie haven't left the room or even talked about leaving, so I figure they're not as angry at me as I thought they would be. My mind feels so light now. Almost all of the sandbags have been emptied.

"Why did you lie to us though? We're your friends, and you could've told us all this when it was happening," Becky says.

"Yeah, now I think I understand everything that seemed so peculiar lately. You've really been holding in some heavy stuff," Janie says.

"You're still speaking to me? I was scared you'd be so angry I lied to you you'd both leave and never speak to me again."

"Nah, we made a pact to stick together, and that'll never be broken on my side at least," Becky says and puts her arm around me. Janie gets on my other side and does the same thing.

"You guys are the greatest. I feel so much better. Let's party." I go over to my CDs and put on a catchy new one. We all start to dance around like crazy and soon start jumping on the bed, too. Jumping up and down with my friends, I feel my cares fly away, and I'm back to being plain old Carolyn Samuels.

But after Becky and Janie have gone to sleep, I lay awake remembering an important thing I haven't told them. They don't know about Jennifer's bulimia and how it might be destroying her life.

My phone rings the next morning, and it's Jennifer.

"Carolyn, I'm so nervous about this afternoon. Do you know what I did last night?"

No, please don't tell me. I don't want to know. It feels so good to have nothing on my mind. But Jennifer doesn't stop.

"Okay, tell me what you did."

"I sneaked into the kitchen when everyone was asleep. You know Brad and I went out last night, but I didn't eat anything; and from not eating anything at lunch, I was starved. I opened up the refrigerator, and the rest of the pizza was there. There were five slices left, and I ate all of them. Then I grabbed the potato chips and stuffed a whole bag into my mouth. I opened the tortilla chips and a jar of salsa, and they were both empty in a few minutes. I mean I hadn't eaten for days. My coach was weighing me every morning. So after that, I just grabbed anything that might be food. Then I swear I didn't make it happen, but I had to run to the bathroom and get rid of it all. I mean, I did feel sick, and maybe I put my finger down my throat a little but not a lot."

My mind is swirling. Did she call me to make me feel guilty? Were we really friends, or was she using me for some bizarre reason I couldn't figure out. I don't want to know all this. Why doesn't she tell her parents? I decide to get Jennifer to tell her parents about her bulimia once and for all. But how can I do it? Should I tell Becky and Janie? Will they keep it a secret? I rack my brain thinking about how I can tell them this.

"So how do you feel today?"

"Not so good and very weak. I'm afraid to eat anything, or it'll all come up again. I need my strength for the meet this afternoon."

"You should try to eat something small like toast or something." I'm not her mother, and I hate this role.

"Yeah, maybe. I'll see if I can get something down before I have to go. You're going to the meet right?"

"Yes, I'm going to be sitting with Becky and Janie. Good luck. I know you'll do great. What do you say to a gymnast?"

"Good luck is fine. It's not like the stage. There you have to say 'break a leg.' If you're a gymnast, that's the biggest disaster that can happen. I guess you can say 'keep your resin dry.'"

"Okay, see you at the meet. Keep your resin dry."

Hanging up the phone, I get this strange feeling of uneasiness. I've got to tell Becky and Janie about Jennifer as soon as possible. I'm going to need more than me to help her. I wonder if any of Jennifer's old friends know about her problem.

Becky and Janie woke when the phone rang, and they're sitting up in their sleeping bags.

"Morning Carolyn," Becky says and gives me a smile as sunny as the rays that peek in through my curtains and land on each girl's hair.

"I'm starved," Janie says, and all three of us go down to the kitchen to see what's for breakfast.

Mom is at her usual place with her coffee and crossword puzzle, but in front of her, in the center of the table is a big platter filled with bagels and bowls of cream cheese, jelly, and lox.

"I didn't know what you'd like, so I put out everything. Help yourselves girls.

I take half a bagel and spread it lightly with cream cheese. I don't have much of an appetite after listening to Jennifer's experience. But having Mom home is the best. She's not too busy on her computer, and she's been home every night. The house looks so much better, and it helps me to know she's there in case I need to talk with her. Maybe this is one of those times.

"Mom, do you have a few minutes?"

"Sure, Carolyn, but aren't you with your friends now?"

"Guys, I really have to talk with my mom after breakfast. Do you think maybe you can find something to do for a few minutes? You can play on my computer. I have a new game."

"Sure, Carolyn, we'll be upstairs."

When breakfast is over, and Becky and Janie have gone upstairs to my room, I sit down at the table next to Mom.

"Mom, you remember Jennifer right? Well you know that day when she fainted in school? It was because she was weak from not eating. She does that. She either doesn't eat, or she eats a lot and throws it up. She's been doing it since middle school."

"Honey, that sounds terrible. Oh, now I understand about the morning we drove her to school." She looks at me with her eyes trained on mine. "Do her parents know about her?" I shake my head. "Maybe she should tell them. Go on, I can see you have more to tell me."

Mom sits there as calm as can be, and I continue. You'd think she was hearing about the weather or something. "Well, you know she's in this gymnastic meet this afternoon. I've helped her this week. I did her homework for her, and she paid me. Do you think that's wrong?" I wait for the volcano to erupt. Mom's expression changes a little, but it's not up to her boiling point, so I continue. "Also, this isn't the only time. I did it for her the first night of school. It's just in math, but it helped her to have more time with her boyfriend, because she had to practice so much. This way she could see him after school."

Her face gets all red and puffy like she's going to explode. Now she looks like she's about to boil over. Uh, oh, I've gone too far.

"Carolyn," Mom fumes at me, "you did someone's homework for money?"

"Yes," I whisper almost under my breath.

"You did Jennifer's homework so she could spend time with her boyfriend? What were you thinking? What if you got caught? Think of how you'd feel. I'd have had to go into the office and speak with the principal. They might fail you in the class. Where were your brains?"

"I don't know." My tongue and mouth are dry as sandpaper. I get up and reach for a bottle of water in the fridge.

"What did you use the money for? If you had money, why did you ask me for some last night?"

"I didn't have the money then. Jennifer gave it to me so I could get this dress we liked for the Homecoming Dance."

"You didn't tell me you were going to any dance. Do you have a date?"

"Not exactly, but Jennifer is trying to fix me up with one of Brad's friends. You remember Brad. He's on the football team, quarterback."

"I think I do, but Carolyn, this could have gotten you kicked off the cheerleading team. Don't do it again. Do I make myself clear? And how much did this dress cost?"

"Um, two hundred and fifty-five dollars."

Mom hears this in stony silence. Then I see I've really set her off with this last statement.

Her eyes open wide. "Are you out of your mind? I mean I've made a little more money this month, but not that much more. You can't spend this amount on one dress. It's out of the question."

I hate my Mom at this moment and burst into tears.

"I didn't really want the dress, but Jennifer insisted. I mean I don't really have a date for the dance and…" I can't continue, but I have to tell Mom about my crush on Brad. "Mom…listen…um…you know Brad…well, maybe I kind of like him."

I break down completely then, and Mom comes over and puts both her arms around me. A lot of people have been doing this since yesterday. I'm really getting to be a basket case. Max comes up to me with his tail wagging and pushes himself under my arm. I pet his soft head.

"Carolyn, I had no idea about this. You know what? If you put money on the dress, it will keep, and we'll think about it. What are you going to do about this boy?"

"I kind of thought you might help me with this one. I don't want to break up Jennifer and her boyfriend, but Brad and I have become friends, and he's so nice. I don't know what to do. Now Jennifer wants us all to go out on a date at the dance. You know Mom I've never been on a real date. I'm so scared and don't know what to do. I don't want to go back to the way things were with Jennifer and me last year. Help me, please."

I'm still kind of teary, and Mom gives me a tissue to wipe my face. "I can't do much for you except tell you to do the right thing."

"How will I know what the right thing is?"

"When the time comes, you'll know. These things have a way of working themselves out without you doing a thing."

What kind of answer is that? Now I have so many more questions and no answers. But strangely I feel better having told my mom everything. It's going to be easier to tell Becky and Janie after this about Jennifer.

"She's bulimic?" Becky says. "That explains a lot of stuff to me. There was this program on TV about kids who were either bulimic or anorexic. Did you know you can be both at the same time?" Becky always seems to know about stuff like this.

"You've known about this since the night you went over to her house, and you didn't tell anyone until today? Did you tell your mom?" Janie can't believe I can hold in such a secret for so long.

"Actually I told her just before I told you guys, but I told you about my crush on Brad before her so we're even." I smile at my friends.

"Now I don't know if I can face Jennifer knowing what I know, but it certainly explains a lot of stuff about her. Don't you go getting like her, though. I heard people who are close to bulimics can become bulimic themselves." Becky warns me.

This is news to me. I wonder if it's contagious, like a disease. Will I get it?

"They can? Do you think I'll get that way?"

Becky looks at me like I'm insane.

"Also," she continues, "I found out in the same program it affects your skeleton. People who have it can have weaker bones and tooth problems among other things."

"Becky, how do you remember all this stuff?"

"You know I have a poem that was written by a girl who is bulimic. Do you want to see it? I'll have my mom email it to me. I have it on my computer." Becky won't stop talking about this.

"Sure, but you don't have to do it today. I can see it tomorrow. Don't give any more work to your mom. Doesn't she have enough taking care of your twin brothers?"

"It's very scary to see how this girl feels. Do you think Jennifer feels like this?" I'm sure Becky is just curious, but I've probably told everyone enough.

"I don't know. I've had some talks with her about it, but I don't think it would be right to tell you what she said. I feel bad enough telling you about it. Please don't let her know. If you do, I'll be toe jam again to her."

"Don't worry, we won't," Janie says. We all start getting dressed to go to the gymnastic meet.

Chapter Twenty-Three

Mom pulls up to the school, and we join the crowd pouring into the gym. The bleachers are set up, and we take a seat in front, so we'll be able to see everything going on in the gym. The gymnasts have to go from station to station, and they rotate by teams. We're right in front of the balance beam. On the floor are a set of uneven parallel bars, a large blue mat, a wooden horse, and a set of rings hanging from the ceiling. I notice a big box of a white powder near each of the stations. This must be the resin box.

Curtained areas with different colors line the sides of the gym. Benches have been set up in front of the curtains, and each team is now sitting on each of the benches. I see Jennifer with her team, and she looks very pale. In fact, she looks as bad as the day she fainted. She smiles at me, and I wave to her. She waves back, and I mouth "Good luck."

The meet begins with singing the national anthem, and the announcer explains what will happen and the rules. The participants will add points to their team score, but individuals will be competing for points as well. Every person will rotate through each station, and at the end of the meet, the scores will be tallied. The teams start at the same time, and I don't know where to look. Jennifer's team starts at the mat, and each girl does a routine for about three minutes.

Jennifer's routine is spectacular. Her somersaults are breathtaking, and she does perfect cartwheels. In between the gymnastic moves, her dancing flows smoothly, and she ends with a quadruple somersault across the whole mat. She stands there with her hands up in the air, and I know she's gotten a great score. The cards the judges hold up confirm Jennifer has the best score of everyone on her team for this element.

The whole team rotates to the balance beam, and Jennifer gets up after three of her teammates have gone. Seeing her near the beam, I remember my dream, but I feel sure everything is going to be all right. Jennifer dips her feet into the resin and rubs it onto her legs, too. She's covered in white when she steps onto the beam. Jennifer seems to be born to be on a balance beam. She performs all of her routine effortlessly.

At one point during a double somersault, I hold my breath. But she lands on her feet and continues to move along the beam. I'm breathing a sigh of relief when I notice she has slowed down, and her routine is coming to an end. Jennifer moves her right foot over her left foot, and for some reason, the foot doesn't quite get onto the beam. Instead it rests a little to the right of where it should be, and without any warning Jennifer is toppling off the beam to the mat. She lands with her leg in a strange sideways position, and the crowd lets out that sound people make when anyone has an accident in public. It's an 'ah' and 'oh' at the same time. I put my hands to my mouth and scream. This is my dream all over again. I wonder if Jennifer will be able to walk.

The authorities rush to Jennifer, and everything else stops all over the gym as the gymnasts look to where she is being worked on. Jennifer grimaces when they touch her leg, and then two men are holding her up, and she's hopping back to the bench. Everyone applauds and the meet continues. When someone falls off the beam, they have a chance to get back up and continue if they are given the go ahead by the team doctor. This time Jennifer can't continue.

The doctor works on her foot, and soon it's in a soft cast, and she's being wheeled off the floor. *Where are they taking her? Will she go to the hospital? Is her mother or father here?* I don't see them, but I do see her housekeeper, who is right beside Jennifer as they wheel her out of the gym. Her mother and father couldn't come to see her in this big gymnastic meet? Jennifer's coach is looking like he's lost his last dime as she leaves the room. He frowns at the person who goes next.

I can't sit here anymore. I tell Becky and Janie I'll call them and go to see how Jennifer is. Walking out of the gym, I see Brad on the other side of the wheelchair. I run up to Jennifer, and she turns to see me. Tears are streaming down her face, and she looks as pale as an eggshell.

"Jennifer, I saw the whole thing. How do you feel?" I put my hand on her shoulder and feel her trembling.

"How would you feel if you knew your gymnastic career is over?" Jennifer wipes her eyes with the sleeve of her sweatshirt. Now I know she's really miserable. She goes ballistic if even a drop of water gets onto her outfit. What else is going to change about Jennifer? She looks so vulnerable now, and I feel a tug of pain for her.

"There'll be other times and other meets. This isn't the only time you can do this."

"Carolyn," Jennifer looks right into my eyes. "You know that isn't true, but thank you anyway. I've missed my chance. I'm a has-been at fourteen!"

I rub her shoulders and can't find the words to answer her. She could be right. But the cheerleader in me won't let her give up now. I turn to Brad, who's been listening to us and staying silent.

"What do you think about Jennifer's chances for the Olympics?"

Brad kneels down in front of Jennifer and puts his arms around her. She leans her head toward him, and he says, "I think Jen can do whatever she has to do to get to the Olympics, if it's what she wants."

"Oh, Brad, you always make me feel so good. I do feel like maybe I can get through this. The doctor isn't sure if it's broken. So maybe it will heal, and maybe I will have a chance if I can get myself back in shape in time for the next meet in a couple of months."

I find I'm hoping Jennifer gets through this, too. I know how hard she's worked and how disappointed she feels.

"You know, Brad, I'm not sure I'll be able to go to the dance with you next week," Jennifer says as she stares into his eyes.

"Don't say that now. If you can't go I won't either." Brad stands and holds Jennifer's hand. Jennifer keeps looking into his eyes as if they were able to mend her broken body.

"But you're the quarterback, and you've got to go to the dance. Let me figure out a way you can go. It's too late to ask anyone else, but would you accept a substitute I pick for you?" Those eyes must have given her strength because she's smiling now and almost back to her old self.

Brad looks back at her and asks, "How do you know you can't go? They haven't even x-rayed your leg yet. I can't imagine going with anyone but you." Brad's whole face looks like it has fallen about two feet.

Just then Jennifer's face brightens. "I've got it," she looks like she will jump right out of the wheelchair. "How about Carolyn? Oh, this is such a brilliant idea. Carolyn can go in my place. I mean she doesn't really know Jason, so it's not like he'll even be bothered by this. You can find him another date but not Maura. They were like oil and water." Jennifer bounces up and down in her wheelchair.

"Watch it, Jen. Should you be doing that?" Brad gets a concerned look on his face.

"Don't worry, and I'm feeling so much better. You know I was so miserable about not being able to go to the dance. I got this killer dress, and I was looking forward to being there with you." Jennifer closes her eyes. "You'd be there in your new suit, and I would be wearing my new flower dress." She has this faraway look in her eyes.

I can picture her and Brad at the dance and see Jennifer twirling in her new dress. The vision is so vivid I'm surprised to hear my name.

"Carolyn, what do you think of my plan?" *What do I think of it?* I want to jump up and down and scream with Becky and Janie about this. How did it happen? One minute I'm being fixed up with my fake crush and dreading the dance, and now I'm going with Brad, maybe. We're still not sure Jennifer can't go to the dance.

"This is only in case Jennifer can't go, but would you go with me, Carolyn? It would really help me out, and there's no one I'd rather go with besides Jennifer." My heart skips a beat, and I'm warm all over. It starts in my cheeks and moves to my eyes and finally it feels like the top of my head is going to come off. I touch my hair to make sure it's still there.

I look over at Jennifer and nod yes to Brad. I don't trust my own voice now at all. And of course, I can barely breathe. Afraid I'll hyperventilate and faint in front of the two of them I croak out, "See you, have to go." I rush through the gym doors, praying Mom or Dad is outside waiting for me in the car.

Chapter Twenty-Four

"Hi, Carolyn." Brad's voice booms over the phone the next day.

"Hi, Brad," I say, my voice cracking a little.

"Well, the doctor told Jennifer she can't even leave the house for a whole week. Her ankle is broken, and some of her leg muscles have been hurt. She has to rest her leg, and then the doctor will decide next week when she can even walk."

"Oh, that's awful for her. She really wanted to go to the dance. How is she doing?" In my head, I'm saying, *Yes, yes, yes!!*

"How do you think she felt? She can't even stand. I suppose she could go in a wheelchair, but she didn't want to."

I wonder why she didn't want to at least show up for the dance.

"So I guess you're going to be my date for the dance." His voice goes down as if he has resigned himself to it. "Are you okay with it?

I'm glad he's on the phone and not in front of me. My face in the mirror is bright red. How embarrassing would that be? "Sure, I think it's probably the best idea. You do need to go to the dance." I clutch the phone to my ear and pray Brad can't hear my heartbeat through the receiver.

"So what color is your dress, so I can get you flowers that won't clash?"

It's beginning to feel real when he talks about the flowers he's getting me. I breathe in and out way too fast, and soon I'm starting to feel lightheaded and faint.

"My...dress...is...light...blue." My mouth feels like I've swallowed cotton balls, and I can't get a decent breath. Now I'll have to tell Mom and ask her for the extra money. Will she let me get that dress?

"Great, that'll be easy. I was hoping it wouldn't be purple or yellow. It's so hard to match those colors."

"See…you…in…school…on…Monday." I barely manage to get this out.

"Are you okay?" Brad sounds worried on the other end.

I try to sound as normal as possible. But my breathing is getting choppier, so I gasp out, "S...s-s-sure. It's nothing. I'm running upstairs." Will Brad believe that?

"Well as long as you're okay. I have to go. I've got to call Jason and explain this whole mess to him. He was kind of looking forward to meeting you and taking you to the dance." Brad couldn't be telling me the truth. The guy doesn't even know me.

When I hear that, though, my breathing calms, and I say goodbye to Brad. When I hang up, the phone rings again immediately.

"Carolyn, hi." Jennifer is probably trying to find out if Brad called me. I'm feeling slightly guilty, but it's her idea, right?

"Hi, Jen," I say. "How are you feeling?"

"Not so great. The doctor told me I can't even stand on the leg this whole week. Mom got me a wheelchair. But I pretty much have to be in bed or on the sofa all week. He won't let me go to the dance, except in a wheelchair."

"How come you don't want to go to the dance in a wheelchair?"

"No wheelchair for me. You know how active I am. Well, can you imagine me watching everyone dance? I'm not crippled, and I can give up one dance. Anyway, you'll be there to keep Brad company."

I marvel at how Jennifer has such optimism. Probably comes from years of people fawning over her. Wish I had her confidence. Then I wonder what I will wear to the dance

"Jennifer, can I do your homework for you this week?" What am I doing?

"Sure, but why? I'll have plenty of time to do it now. I mean what else can I do but homework?"

"Yeah, I know, but now I've kind of got to do it. Don't make me beg...oh, all right, I'm begging. I really, really need the money for my dress." Mom will probably ground me for the rest of my life if she finds out I'm doing Jennifer's homework for money, but can I ask her for that amount of money? Maybe I should ask her anyway.

"Well, if you need the money, then of course go ahead and do it. Of course, I could pay you, and you wouldn't have to do anything for me."

"You know on second thought, I might ask my mom for the money after all. But keep that option open for me, okay?" I remember how I felt the last time I lied to Mom. Could I go back to the sandbags in my head?

"You know with all this talk about a dress, it sounds like Brad called you."

"Yes, actually he just called me. That's how I knew about your leg. I'm so sorry. Are you in a lot of pain?"

"No, the doctor gave me these great pain pills, but they make me tired. So I may have to get off soon."

"Okay. Do you want to get off now?"

"No. Actually I wanted to find out if Brad's going to tell Jason about not having a date for the dance?"

"Yes, he's going to call him and explain the whole thing. Brad said Jason has been looking forward to meeting me, but I didn't believe him."

"Oh, my God, Carolyn! What is wrong with you? Do you ever give yourself a break?" There's silence on the other end. Is Jennifer angry with me?

"It's just I've never had a boy interested in me at all, and now to have two of them want to be with me…"

"You have no idea what you look like, do you?"

I realize this is something she can't possibly have experienced. She probably had a boyfriend from the time she was two. We can never understand each other. I see the gap between us like the space between two buildings that can never quite be jumped. I can feel myself about to fall, and I get that "can't breathe" feeling with her for the first time in weeks.

"Uh, Jennifer, I have to go now." I can feel myself begin to pant. There's a funny quiet at the other end.

"Carolyn, are you doing that breathing thing again? Why don't you calm down and try to act a little cooler? You'll be a nervous wreck if you don't chill a little."

"I'm really nervous about Saturday night, you know. It's like my first real date, and I don't know what to do. I mean you've been dating for years. Can you give me some little hints on what I should do?"

Jennifer launches into her favorite subject, boys. She gives me a whole spiel like I was reading *Dating for Dummies*.

"Carolyn, the first thing is what to wear. I always feel what you're wearing helps you to feel good about yourself. So what are you going to wear?"

I think back to our shopping trip and the beautiful blue dress we found and put on layaway. "Remember that dress we found when we went shopping together for you? I guess I could wear it. Also, I have plenty of money now to pay for it." If I ask Mom, or do Jennifer's homework, but I must have that dress.

"That's right, it's perfect. Do you have shoes to go with it?"

I didn't have shoes or a bag to go with the dress. I'd have to persuade my mom to take me to the mall. Maybe Becky or Janie could come with me. I know I'd feel more comfortable with one of them instead of Jennifer. "No, but I'll get them before Saturday. I'll get my mom to take me to the mall."

Jennifer makes a choking sound. "Carolyn, are you sure you want to do that?"

I run the scene in my mind. Me and Mom at the mall. What was I thinking?

"You're right, of course. I'm so nervous my brain cells are starting to disintegrate. Mom at the mall will be a nightmare. She and I never agree on anything, and with shoes it's worse. Last time I went shopping with her, we didn't speak to each other for two days. She made me buy shoes even geeks wouldn't wear. I hid them in my closet and never wore them."

Jennifer laughs.

"She hardly noticed with her busy schedule. I mean, who looks at anyone's feet anyway?" I check the hall quickly to see if Mom is within earshot of this. But it's clear, and my secret's still safe.

"See what I mean? Go with Becky and Janie. Hey, I have an idea. You can pick up the dress and bring it with you to buy the shoes." Jennifer has that I'm-so-pleased-with-myself voice again.

It's getting late, and I realize I still have to do my homework.

"Jen, I have to go now. Thank you for all the great advice, and I'm beginning to think I might not fall on my face at this dance after all." I laugh into the phone, and Jennifer laughs back. Are we really becoming friends?

"Okay, but stay cool, and I'll see you tomorrow. Come by the house. I won't be at school for a whole week. Mom is telling my teachers. On Friday, the doctor's making me come to the office to get my leg checked. Then he'll decide if I have to be off of it for longer. That sucks doesn't it?"

"Yeah, but think of your career. Rest it now, so it'll be okay. We'll get together tomorrow. I'll try to get over to your house. Maybe I'll take the bus after school and get dropped off there."

"Sure, whatever." She starts to sound a little drowsy, and I have to go anyway.

"Bye, Jen. Again, thanks for everything. You've been great to me." *Don't gush,* I say to myself. You're being ridiculous.

"Night, talk to you tomorrow." Jen hangs up.

I head to my desk and start my homework. But I can't really concentrate, because the blue dress keeps popping into my head and overtakes the page, erasing the math problem. All I can think about is getting the dress and the shoes to match it. How shallow have I become?

Chapter Twenty-Five

Jennifer isn't in school the next morning, and I realize I miss her. John and I have become "really friends," and he gives me a big smile when I get to my seat. It takes me awhile, because all the kids stop me to ask about Jennifer. Suddenly I'm the center of attention. Even when Mr. Armbruster begins the class, kids stage whisper to me with their hands cupped over their mouths.

"How's Jennifer? Tell her Amy said hello."

Have I become Jennifer's personal assistant now? My dream is sorta coming true, but it's more of a nightmare. No one cares about me. It's all Jennifer, Jennifer. Who was I kidding? I'll never be like Jennifer Taylor, even if I do go out with Brad. I mean, won't he be comparing me to her all night?

Suddenly the whole dance thing scares me, and I get a breathing attack.

"Carolyn, what's wrong? You're turning blue. Are you okay?" John swivels in his seat to check me out.

"I, uh, uh, get, uh, this, uh, way some, uh times." I am practically panting like a dog that's been running for a mile. This is getting worse. I don't have anyone to calm me down.

Jennifer would have told me to snap out of it. Becky and Janie would have soothed me. John doesn't know what to do. He looks like a puppy who's lost his chew toy,

"Can I do anything for you?" John kneels down to ask me.

I can't answer him. It's too late. I know I'll faint if I don't do this. Bending in half, I put my head between my legs and look at the upside down face of Mr. Armbruster in back of me.

"Ms. Samuels are you practicing a cheer for us?"

The whole class laughs.

I'm looking at my loafers and can't raise my head.

"No," I pant to him. Can't he see I need help?

"Sit up, or you'll get detention."

He's commanding me now.

I try to raise my head. Tiny polka dots swim before my eyes. There's a haze over the math room. I manage to get my head to my desktop and collapse there. Mr. Armbruster's expression changes. There's actual concern.

"Are you having trouble breathing?"

I can only nod my head. No words come from my mouth. It's too busy trying to get air.

"You need the nurse. Can you get there by yourself?"

Does he think I can even move from this seat? I shake my head no.

"Mr. Sumner, would you please escort Ms. Samuels to the nurse?"

John gets out of his seat and helps me out of mine.

"Sure, Mr. Armbruster." He leads me out of the math room and down the hall.

The nurse's office is close to the gym, and by the time I arrive there, I'm feeling better. My breathing is back to normal.

"John, I'm fine. You can leave."

"Darn," he says. "I get a chance to hang out with one of the only smart cheerleaders in the school and skip math, and you tell me I can leave." He gives me a big grin.

Somehow this makes me feel even better, and I'm wondering what it would be like to be with John walking me to my next class, when the nurse sees him.

"Guess I've gotta go now."

"Thanks for taking me here. I'll see you tomorrow." I give him a smile, and he smiles back. Something about that smile gives me a warm feeling all through my body.

He gets a pass from the nurse and waves to me as he saunters out of the nurse's office.

I wave back and sit on one of those hideous mattresses.

The nurse comes right over to me. It's not busy, only one girl lying on the first Naugahyde mattress.

"Carolyn, nice to see you," the nurse says.

She must remember me from when Jennifer had her problems.

"Mr. Armbruster called me on the intercom about your breathing problem."

She takes out her stethoscope and checks me. Then she takes my pulse, and I'm feeling like an idiot. Nothing's wrong.

Should I tell her about the other times? Might as well. It'll get me out of math class.

The nurse is ahead of me, though.

"Has this happened to you before today?"

When I nod my head, yes, she continues.

"Tell me how you felt before it happened."

"I don't know. Sometimes I'll be sitting somewhere, and I'll be thinking, and suddenly I'll have problems breathing."

"How long has this been happening?" The nurse arches her eyebrows and looks at me.

"I guess the first time was in middle school when I was going into a big test. Now," and I pause and look her straight in the eyes, "it happens every time I get nervous. Once I even fainted, and I was in this office to get checked; but that was the first day of school, and you couldn't see me. Remember the food poisoning day? My gym teacher sent me."

But the nurse has walked away from me. I'm talking to air. She comes back with paper bags.

"You're hyperventilating. It happens to older people, too. Next time you feel this way, blow into a paper bag, not plastic or you'll suffocate yourself. You open it up and place it over your mouth and nose. You can use these."

She hands me the paper bags.

"Keep a few with you at all times, just in case."

She stops talking and walks over to the girl lying down. She puts her hand on the girl's forehead and pops a thermometer into the girl's mouth.

I get up to leave, and the nurse is already writing my pass.

"Go back to class. You're okay. Remember the paper bags."

Mom always has a lot of those paper lunch bags. I guess they're left over from when I brought my lunch to school.

I wish those days were back. It was easy then, although I didn't think so. Just Becky, Janie, and me, and we all hated Jennifer. Now life is so complicated, and I have a new embarrassment. I've got to put a paper bag over my face to breathe. Will my life ever be normal?

I run into Becky on the way to my next class.

"What are you carrying those bags for?" I realize I'm clutching the bags in my hand.

"I had a breathing attack in math, and the nurse gave them to me. Actually, I almost fainted again, like the first day in gym.

"You should see a doctor."

"No, I don't need to. The nurse said I'm hyperventilating, whatever that means."

Then I realize I have to tell Becky about John.

"Becky, you know the cute guy I told you about in math? He's always kidding around with Jennifer and me? Mr. Armbruster asked him to take me to the nurse. If I didn't like Brad so much, he'd be a close second."

"Really? You mean there's someone our age you might like?"

"Well, I don't know how I feel about him, but he's funny, and he's got a great smile."

"Sounds like we have to talk more at lunch. Before I go, I've got to know. What are you supposed to do with those bags?"

"Put them over my mouth and nose to help stop the attack. But I haven't tried it yet, so I can't tell you if it works. All I know is I've got to stop these attacks, or I'll go out of my mind."

"Yeah, and we wouldn't want a repeat of 'breathe, Carolyn breathe' for this semester. I mean, have you seen the way Maura looks at you, me, and Janie at lunch?"

I look over at my best friend and see the pain in those honest eyes. Why should she have to suffer because of me? Why did I drag my friends into my nightmare? This Friday we won't be having our usual Chinese food for lunch. At Jennifer's table, everyone gets the school lunch. I feel homesick for my old table and my old life. But I am too far into Jennifer's life to stop now. Becky turns to go to her last class before lunch when the bell rings.

"See you at lunch, Becky. I miss our Fridays. Don't you?" It's only Monday, but I'm wishing this week would end.

"Yeah, I wish we could all go back and sit at our usual table. Maybe we'll do that soon. I don't have fun at lunch anymore. You are better, right? See you at lunch." She gazes into my eyes to check to see if I'm okay and then gives my shoulder a little squeeze.

"I'm better." I grab her arm to keep her from leaving. "You're not angry at me are you? You know how I feel about Maura. When she looks at me, it's like hearing chalk squeak on a blackboard. She's one of those people who should have a warning sign before she speaks."

Becky laughs and waves goodbye.

Through the next period, I think about lunch. What will it be like without Jennifer there? Will Brad be friendly to me? How will Maura act?

Chapter Twenty-Six

Lunch passes easily to my surprise. Maura is absent today, and Brad comes to the table with his usual pizza. He smiles over at me, and a warm glow creeps all over my body starting at my cheeks. The dance is only five days away, and I'm looking forward to it.

"Hey, Carolyn, how're you doing today?" Brad grabs a slice of pizza with our favorite pepperoni and takes a giant bite.

"Hi, Brad, I'm great. How're you?" Inside I'm a wreck. But I'm managing to keep things together for the time being.

He mumbles something that sounds like great. Then I realize his mouth is full of pizza, and he can't talk.

"Did you understand what I said? The pizza looked so good I just bit into it at the same time you talked to me. Sorry. I said I feel great, too." He continues to eat his pizza, and in a few bites, it's finished.

I haven't eaten a bite of my lunch, which happens to be the same as his. I start eating the salad that goes along with lunch.

"Do you want that pizza?" Brad moves his puppy dog eyes over to my slice. Suddenly I know I won't eat more than salad. The blue dress hanging in my closet helps me make up my mind.

"No, do you want it Brad?" I pass my tray over to him, and he takes it.

"Good thing we both like the same thing on our pizza." As if we had a choice here. Every time we have pizza, there's only plain or pepperoni.

Minutes go by with neither of us talking. In fact, it's silent at the table. No one is saying anything. Maybe everyone is wishing Jennifer were here instead of me. Is Brad wishing that, too? I wonder will he get bored at the dance with me as his date? What will I say to him? I can't flirt like Jennifer. And I don't know much about football. I guess I could look into his eyes and hope he talks to me first. What if he doesn't? How will I do this? I get anxious and pray I don't have a breathing attack in front of Brad. How embarrassing would that be?

"Carolyn," I practically leap out of my seat when my name is mentioned.

"Becky, you scared me half to death. Did you know that?" I give my friend a smile as I say this to tell her it's okay.

"Hey, all I wanted was to tell you it's almost gym time. Maybe I should have tapped you on the shoulder. Then you'd really be scared. Sorry." She looks uncomfortable, and I know it is not what she's done but me. I am going berserk, and it is all 'cause of this dance. I move closer to Becky. I'm glad that without Jennifer there, I won't have to cope with her table alone.

"Come with me to the bathroom, please." I whisper into Becky's ear as we sit together. We both get up at the same time, and I tell Brad we'll be back soon.

"Can't you girls ever go to the bathroom alone? What do you do in there, I wonder? Sometimes I wish I had a camera that could film what goes on in the girls' bathroom." Brad laughs, and we go to the bathroom to talk.

"You couldn't talk to me at the table? What is so important we have to talk in private?" Becky faces me with her I-want-an-answer face.

"Well, I was thinking I don't know what to talk to Brad about when I'm at the dance. What do you say to a boy on a date?" Will Becky know and help me, or will I have to call Jennifer and confess that I don't know what to do on a date?

"What makes you think I know what to do? I've never been on a date either."

Becky is trying, but I see she can't help me.

"I don't know. Maybe it's because you have older brothers, and you know how boys think."

Becky puts her lips together and scrunches up her eyes. It's her thinking position.

In a couple of minutes, she opens her eyes and gives a big yell. Luckily no one else is in the bathroom, or we'd have a lot of explaining to do.

"Carolyn, I remember when my brother Johnny was talking to Joey the other day." Besides her twin brothers, she has two stepbrothers: Johnny who's in college and Joey who is a junior here. Becky has always felt strange being the only girl in her family. Now maybe it might be worth it to have brothers. "Johnny was telling Joey he didn't like girls who talk a lot. You know, girls who go on and on and never shut up. Johnny said he would never date anyone like that. Joey said he liked girls who paid attention to what he said. In his words, girls who didn't listen to him weren't worth a second thought. So maybe this will help you to know what to do." Becky has this satisfied smile on her face like a teacher who finds out her whole class has done their homework.

"That's great, Becky. I won't have to change a thing about myself. You know what I'm like around boys. But don't I have to talk a little bit? Should I ask him about football? What do you think?" Becky scrunches her eyes again and concentrates.

"Wear a great dress, don't talk too much, and when he talks, listen like you're going to have a test on everything he says." Then she smiles, and I hug her. This is the perfect advice. Why am I so worried? When I walk out of the bathroom with Becky, I feel lighter. I start planning my trip to the mall.

"Becky, come with me to the mall today. I have to pick up my dress and buy shoes and everything to go with it."

Becky twists herself to look at me.

"You've already bought your dress? How could you have done it so quickly?" She peers into my eyes to get the truth. They drill themselves into my brain, and I can't hide anything from her any longer.

"Well, when I went to the mall with Jennifer to shop for her dress before she had her accident, we found this fantastic dress, and I put some money on it to put it on layaway. I was supposed to go to the dance with Jason Wadsworth the Third, so I needed a dress anyway. Wait until you see it. It's so perfect. And it's blue. You know how I love blue."

"Wait a minute. You already had a date for the dance? You got a dress without me?" Becky stares back at me with confusion.

"We were there, and Jennifer kind of pushed me to get it. You don't know how long I've kept this from you. It's been weeks. But today I realized I can't continue keeping the truth from you and Janie." Damn I'm starting to cry now, and I'm worried I won't be able to continue. I feel lower than the sole of my shoe right now. I wipe my eyes with my fingers.

We get to the lunch table, but the bell rings, and we have to go to gym. Brad looks across at me and winks. It makes me feel all tingly and much better, but I still have to face Becky and Janie with the truth of everything. Now I've started I want to get it all out. I've got to suck all the poison out of me.

"I'll call you tonight, and we'll get all of our plans straight for the dance, okay? I want to remind myself of the color of your dress and everything. I'll call you about sevenish. Talk to you later." Brad leaps up from the table like he's about to make a run across the lunchroom, but he starts walking normally toward the door. My heart leaps and starts beating uncontrollably. I will myself to keep breathing normally, but when did that ever help? In time, I remember the paper bags and take one and put it over my mouth and nose.

"Are you okay, Carolyn? What do you have over yourself?" Becky runs over to me and sees the paper bag. "Gee, who'd think you'd have to use this so quickly. Is it working?"

I remove the bag and try to breathe normally. Everyone is looking at me like I just had another arm grow out of my body. But I don't care. At least I didn't faint, and no one except Becky really knows why I have a bag over my face. I walk out of the lunchroom holding the bag with one hand and carrying my books with the other. I can't wait to go to the mall this afternoon. My breathing gets better, and I throw the bag away in the first trash basket we come to. Images of my dress and various kinds of shoes float through my mind. I feel a tiny bit better and actually smile at Becky as we push open the locker room doors.

Chapter Twenty-Seven

A week passes much to my surprise, because each day drags, and I think Saturday night will never come. But believe it or not here it is. I'm all ready and don't dare look at myself in the mirror.

Mom passes by in the hall and stops like she's been turned to stone.

"Is this my little girl all dressed up and looking like a princess?" Mom can exaggerate sometimes, and this time she's definitely gone overboard.

"Mom, stop it. I look like I always look, right? I mean how different could I be?"

Mom steps into my room and turns me to face the mirror so I can see myself completely. I don't believe what I look like. Who is this stranger? Pleased to meet you, are you taking the place of Carolyn?

"I guess I do look okay. I mean this dress is amazing, and thank you for the hair appointment today." I hug Mom, and she hugs me, and I start to calm down. This person staring back at me in the mirror looks like she is a calmer version of me.

"You're going to have a great time tonight. Just don't worry about anything. Be natural and be yourself, and everything will be fine." Mom is smiling this gigantic smile, and then she gets another idea.

"I've got to get my camera and take a picture of you. Just wait a minute, I'll be right back." She runs out of my room and comes back a few seconds later with her digital camera.

"Okay, give me a smile." I oblige her, and she takes so many pictures of me I have big spots in front of my eyes from the flash going off.

I'm afraid I'm going to fall down the stairs because I can barely see, and then the doorbell rings. Suddenly it's all real. I'm going out with Brad tonight. I get that no breath feeling and yell at myself.

Carolyn, you have to get a hold of yourself. You can't have a breathing attack now. How would it look if you went to the door with a paper bag on your face? Anyway, where can I keep paper bags? This dress doesn't have pockets. I guess I'll have to fold one of the paper bags up and keep it in my handbag. I pray I won't get an attack with Brad. How embarrassing to faint at a dance.

I start downstairs and see Brad and Dad are busy talking about the stupid football game on TV. As I get to the middle of the staircase, Brad looks up at me. He looks so incredible in a dark suit and crisp white shirt. He keeps staring at me as I walk down each stair slowly, because I'm wearing shoes with a little heel and don't want to trip and fall at his feet. That would be a great way to start my first date ever.

"Wow," both Brad and my dad say together.

"Hi, Brad, you look great." I am barely able to speak at all.

"Carolyn, you look so good. I got you some flowers to go with your dress." Brad hands me a package containing a wrist corsage of beautiful blue flowers that smell amazing. My heart is beating so fast I think I'll have a heart attack if I don't calm down.

"We should go," Brad says looking at me like I'm a Christmas present. I feel all fluttery, and I'm afraid I won't be able to speak at all.

Brad takes my coat and helps me with it. I look at Dad; Mom comes into the room and stands near Dad. Mom takes a picture of Brad and me, and then as we open the door to leave, she and Dad come over and give me a big hug.

"Have a great time and call us if you are going to be later than you said." Mom and Dad stand in the doorway, and it's my turn to get teary. I keep remembering how many times I wished I would be the one going out with the pretty dress and a handsome escort. I feel like I'm in my own Disney movie as Brad helps me into the car and closes the door carefully to protect my dress.

On the ride to the dance, I'm thinking about the reason why I'm here with Brad. My dream has finally come true. I really am like Jennifer Taylor.

Chapter Twenty-Eight

The gym is all decorated, so it looks more like a forest than a gym. There are real colored leaves all over the floor, and crepe paper covers everything. Kids are dancing to a local band playing on a stage. When we walk into the place, everyone looks surprised. As we move past each couple, I can hear the whispering behind us. One girl actually bursts out laughing and pokes her date in the arm as we pass.

"Carolyn, are you okay?" Brad holds my arm and steers me to a table.

"Sure, I'm fine." I lie, because what else can I say.

"Well, I heard those guys talking about us. It didn't bother you, right?

"No, and thanks for that." So far I'm able to talk and breathe at the same time. Brad is so sweet. I can't believe we are really here.

The band starts playing a song, and Brad says, "This is my favorite song. Let's dance, okay?"

We glide onto the dance floor, and I glance up at the streamers above my head.

Brad dances as well as he does everything else. We dance and dance and ignore the stares of the other people there. So far I haven't had to say much of anything. But Brad hasn't talked much either.

The music ends finally, and we go back to the table with a snack and some soda.

Uh oh, I think. Now I'm going to have to say something more.

"You know Carolyn, when Jen suggested you and I come to the dance together, I said it was okay, but I was really miserable."

I nod and say, "I know. Who would want to come with me?"

"No, that's not what I mean. You're great, don't you know that?"

Now I'm worried I'll have a breathing attack, but I try to control myself.

When I don't answer, Brad keeps looking at me, waiting for some words to come out of my mouth.

"Oh, are you waiting for me to say something?"

"Never mind talking now. I wanted to tell you how I felt, because I don't want you to get the wrong idea."

This is it. He's never going to talk to me again after this, I'm sure of it.

"Jen and I have been going out for over a year. She's outstanding, and believe me, I don't have to be going out with a freshman. But she makes me feel so good just to be near her. You know what I mean?"

No, I don't know what he means. I always feel uncomfortable when I'm with her.

"Yeah, well I never thought I'd meet anyone else who can make me feel that good, but I have to tell you, I really like hanging around with you."

Now I'm about to faint. Isn't this a dream? Can it really be happening to me, Carolyn Samuels?

Brad goes on, but I'm getting into a state of breathlessness.

"Yeah, you're like the sister I never had. So what I want to do is, when Jen feels better, I want us to go out on a double date. You know, me and Jen and you and someone."

I hope my expression doesn't show how I feel now. He likes me as a friend, only. Of course, I know I can't compete with Jennifer, and inside I'm crying. The dream is over. If this were a movie, I'd run away leaving Brad with a strange expression on his face. But it's time for me to face facts. Brad and Jennifer belong together. I've always known this, and tonight was the clincher.

I smile at Brad and realize I'm really enjoying myself. "Let's dance. That's a really great song they're playing." I take Brad's hand and lead him to the dance floor. I can't be like Jennifer Taylor, but for tonight I can enjoy the dance with Brad. Tomorrow I'll figure this all out.

Chapter Twenty-Nine

Wow! What a year this has been. I didn't think more could happen, but it did. I thought I liked Brad and everything would end like a fairy tale; but after three years of having a crush on him, when we are finally together at the dance, and we really talk, it is all about Jennifer. We part at the end of the night as friends. It's all so easy, like putting the right pieces into a jigsaw puzzle.

Jennifer and Brad belong together. I'm not the least bit sorry they continue going out. My life changes, too. John and I become friendlier and friendlier, and then one day during lunch our whole relationship changes.

"Hi, Carolyn," John says as I get to my table. Was he here about schoolwork?

"Hi, John. Did you start the assignment yet?" We're working together all the time since the first time I helped him.

He looks at me with his hazel eyes and a guilty little smile.

"You didn't start it did you? Okay, what's your problem?" I am practically scolding him.

"It's not math that's giving me the problem today." He sits next to me, squirming around in his seat a little as if he can't get comfortable.

"So what is causing your problem today?"

"I can't concentrate on anything." He gives me a tight smile.

"So tell me why." I've never seen him so fidgety.

"Let's go outside for a minute, okay?" John stands and motions for me to follow him.

Becky and Janie are still getting their lunch, so I walk outside the lunchroom with John. The hallway is practically deserted.

"Okay, close your eyes, and I'll tell you." This is a weird request, but I do it. Soon I feel hands touching mine. I open my eyes.

John is holding both of my hands and smiling at me. What's going on here?

"John, what are you doing?" I laugh and keep my hands in his. They feel like they belong there.

"Carolyn, haven't you noticed I don't look at anyone else anymore? I've wanted to do this for a long time now. But we're always doing work, and I know you've had a crush on some guy. So I didn't. I don't know, but I decided to do it today." He takes a deep breath.

I wait with my hands still in his. I'm beginning to feel all warm and tingly.

"Do you think maybe you might go out with me sometime? I think we'd have a good time." John lets out his breath slowly and releases my hands.

I'm in shock, and I can't answer because I'm having one of my breathing attacks. John knows all about them now, so I take out my paper bag (I always keep one in my pocket) and lean down a little to blow into it. He laughs and stands in front of me to cover this strange behavior. Pretty soon we go back into the lunchroom. Becky and Janie come back with their lunch as he walks away. All lunch period I can't think of anything else but the feeling of my hands in John's. I've always thought he was cute, but suddenly I can only think of John. I spill my milk, and John looks over at me. We smile at each other. Becky and Janie ask me a lot of questions.

Who's that, Carolyn? Why don't we know him?" Becky has on her what-are–you-pulling-on-us expression.

Janie chimes in with, "Now Carolyn is a cheerleader, she's attracting all the cute guys. So where did you meet him?" Janie emphasizes the word *him*.

"Guys, he's in my math class. We were only friends until now. I mean I thought that's what we were." I stop and gaze into space. The din of the crowded lunchroom melts away for a minute. I'm still a little bit in shock, but then I realize where I am when Becky and Janie start snapping their fingers in front of my eyes.

"Sorry, I'm still recovering. What was I saying? Oh yeah, we were only friends." Peeking over at John for a second, I say, "But I'm not so sure anymore." I look at my two best friends for an answer.

"He wasn't looking at you like a friend. Maybe he's hungry and was looking at the food, but I don't think it's a friend thing." Becky gives me a wink, and I realize how I feel.

After lunch, John looks at me with a question. We walk out of the cafeteria together, and it feels right.

"Well, is it yes or no? If it's yes, how about coming to the movies with me this Friday night?"

I don't have to think at all. "It's yes, and I'd love to go to the movies with you."

John gives my free hand a squeeze and leaves me standing in the hallway as he mouths, "I'll call you."

"Becky, Janie, you'll never guess what just happened! John asked me out for a date.

Friday night!"

"I knew he couldn't be that hungry." Becky and Janie are as excited as I am, and we're jumping up and down when I stop suddenly.

I realize he doesn't know my number, and it's unlisted. So I dash over half of the hallway to him and write it on a piece of loose-leaf paper.

Becky and Janie throw up their hands and laugh.

This is so like me. Then I have to run to make my next class.

For the rest of the day, I can't concentrate at all. I keep wondering when he'll call. Will it be tonight? What will I wear?

When I tell Jennifer and Brad, they're so happy. I feel like I've won a contest.

"Brad," Jennifer says, "this is so great. Now we can double date with Carolyn."

"Look guys, this is only a first date. I mean, we know each other, but I can't think that far." I'm smiling outside, but inside I'm doing leaps and flying in the air.

"Who wouldn't want to go out with you again?" Brad turns and gives me his 'Jennifer' smile, and in spite of my good intentions, my heart does flip-flops. Who could resist that smile? It's so great Jennifer, Brad, and I are friends now.

"Okay, you've convinced me. I'm golden." I laugh and so do Jennifer and Brad. We walk out of school together. Life is sure different for me these days. Who would have thought I'd be walking out of school with Brad and Jennifer?

John and I go to the movies on Friday night, and we have a great time. It seems we like the same kind of movies, scary and full of adventure. We even like our popcorn the same way, with butter and gummy bears. It's not hard to talk with him, and he gives me a hug and a kiss on the cheek. This is only the first of many, many dates that get better and better.

So the year progresses, and it seems to me everything is okay. At least on the surface, but underneath all the problems are still there and percolating.

Jennifer is still bulimic. Her parents take her for help to a counselor who specializes in eating disorders. I hope this person will help her get rid of her problem. I am getting to know Jennifer, and I realize her life is not all that great.

There are even days when I wake up and actually like myself. I am getting thinner, and gradually I wind up replacing all the clothes in my closet with smaller sizes.

Being a cheerleader takes up a lot of my time, and I get to know a lot more people in school. I start to relax and forget about worrying about anything, especially when John and I are together. But I'm not aware of what is coming at all.

It's the last week of real school before we go into the test routine where we only come to school if we have a test that day. Becky, Janie, and I are talking together at lunch. We're not at Jennifer's table, because Maura is there, and we're talking about my birthday sleepover.

"I'm so excited about my sleepover. It's going to be so cool. Mom says I can have at least four people, and I'm thinking of inviting Jennifer."

Becky and Janie crinkle up their eyes and try to smile. I guess they don't think I'm serious.

Jennifer comes walking up to the table where we're sitting and sits next to me without an invitation.

"Hi, Jen. What's up?" I look across at Becky and Janie, and they're both wearing their so-what-does-she-want expression.

"Yeah, hi, Jennifer, how is everything?" Becky doesn't really care, I know, but she's doing it for me.

"Depends on which things you're talking about, right? If you mean how are things going with Brad and me, then things are terrific. But if you mean how are things in general in my life, then I'd have to say parts of it don't exactly shine at this moment." She stops talking and looks at me. "My parents are getting a divorce." Jennifer gets all teary-eyed after this speech.

"Gee, I didn't know, Jennifer," Janie says after she sees me put my arm around Jennifer. I didn't realize I had done this until I found my arm around her. I guess Jennifer is ready to let everyone know she isn't so perfect. Now I feel sorrier for her than I ever did for myself. Does this mean Jennifer is one of us now? How do Becky and Janie feel about her? Do I have to be friends with all of Jennifer's friends? Yuck, that means I'll have to have Maura at my party if I invite Jennifer.

But I don't have to worry, because Becky and Janie come and hug her. Soon all of us are standing in a circle with our arms around each other. I smile inside of myself. We're in the middle of the lunchroom, and everyone can see us. Yet Jennifer doesn't care, and she smiles at me, Becky, and Janie. I guess I can get used to having Maura around as long as I don't have to be alone with her.

"So, Jennifer, you know this Saturday is my birthday, and I'm having a sleepover at my house," I say when we break apart and sit down again. "I'd really like you to be there, too. Becky and Janie are coming, and Mom said I could have four people. Do you want to invite anyone?" I keep my fingers crossed that she won't say Maura. She has so many other friends. Maybe she'll name someone else.

"Well, I think maybe Maura might be fun to have there. She knows a lot of cool games, and she's great at makeup and stuff like that. If that's okay with you, I'll invite her." She looks over at Maura. "There she is at the table. I'll call you after school, okay?"

Jennifer glides over to her usual table where Maura is sitting and staring at the four of us being so chummy. I hope Maura won't be able to come but prepare for the idea she will be there. Then I think of how it will be with Maura, Jennifer, Becky, Janie, and me all there together. Was I crazy? How could this work? Will I be sorry I invited Jennifer after all? Maybe I made a big mistake, and my party will be ruined.

"Look over at Jennifer's table, "Janie says, and Becky moves her head in that direction.

"She's talking to Maura now, and Maura's looking over here with the weirdest expression I ever saw on her face," Becky says.

"Wouldn't you be feeling weird if out of the blue Maura invited you to her party, Becky?" Janie says.

I glance over at Jennifer and Maura and see Maura shake her head no. My heart starts beating faster, and I hope against hope her answer is no. I start gasping.

Jennifer heads over to our table again. That was fast. I thought she was going to call me about it. She has a disappointed look on her face.

"Maura can't come. She has to go to her cousin's birthday party on the same day. But I'll still come." She smiles at me, and I don't want to tell her how relieved I am. I breathe out slowly and crumple the paper bag I've been holding.

"That's fine, Jen. We're going to have a great time. Mom's getting pizza, and we'll have cake and watch movies. I'm excited."

"Maybe I'll bring my makeup, and we'll have a real makeover for everyone."

"Sure, that'll be a lot of fun. After all, we're all going to be sophomores next year. We should have a different look."

"Anyway, Carolyn's parties are always great. Her mom makes the best cookies, and she always has a lot of food. I actually wait all year for her sleepover, "Janie says.

Becky laughs and so do Jennifer and I. The bell rings, and we all drift out of the lunchroom.

I'm feeling better now I've invited Jennifer, and I know Maura isn't coming. I just hope Jennifer doesn't start to feel guilty and go back to her old ways. She's been so good since her parents have put her into counseling. I hope this thing with her parents won't bother

her too much. I wonder how long she's known about the divorce. Maybe I'll call her tonight and find out. I can't believe it's only five more days until the end of school and my sleepover. I can't wait.

Chapter Thirty

Saturday arrives. To my surprise, it's not raining, and everyone is coming to my sleepover tonight. Mom has been out all day getting ready, and I've been getting ready, too. I get up early and clean my room. It's a good thing I do. I find the mates to twelve socks I lost. Also I find three blouses, two different shoes I've been looking for all year, and my science homework I thought I'd lost from November. A pair of cut-offs are stuck between my dresser and the wall, and under the bed are three pieces of un chewed bubble gum in their wrappers. I show Mom, and she says it's nice to see my floor again. Then she smiles and hugs me. It's been a long time since we've hugged. Now it's me who doesn't have the time for her.

"I'm so proud of you, Carolyn. You're turning into a responsible person. I can't wait to tell your father how you cleaned your room top to bottom. He's always telling me he tries to get you to clean, but he loses patience, and I'm too tired when I get home to make you do it. Good for you." She runs downstairs, I guess to call my dad at work. I go back to sorting out the stuff on my desk.

But Mom is back upstairs to tell me I have a phone call. I left my cell phone in my backpack and must have forgotten to turn it off. Mom hands me the phone.

"Hi." I'm thinking it's Jennifer, or Becky or Janie. It could be John. I wanted to invite him, but Mom said, "no boys." So it's going to be an all-girls night.

"Oh, hi." This voice sounds bored and miserable.

"Maura?"

"Yeah, it's me. Listen, Carolyn, I know I told Jennifer I couldn't come because I had my cousin's party, but funny thing…" Maura pauses, and I'm not sure I want to hear what funny thing it is.

"Okay, what funny thing?" I'm losing patience and want to get back to my desk sorting.

"Well, this is the thing, I can come to your birthday sleepover after all. My cousin has the chicken pox, and her party is postponed. So I'm free." I wonder why she's trying to get to my party.

"Um, Maura, why do you want to come anyway? I mean we haven't been good friends this year." I take a deep breath and realize I don't have any trouble breathing. Maura doesn't frighten me anymore.

"I don't know. I don't want to sit home, and it's too late to get a date for tonight, so you're stuck with me." Maura sighs as if she has to walk over hot coals instead of coming to my sleepover.

"Okay, I'll see you at seven-thirty. Do you know where my house is?" A part of me hopes she gets lost and never shows up tonight. But another part wants her to be here for Jennifer so she'll feel more comfortable. Unfortunately, anywhere Maura has been has become a disaster for me. I tell Maura how to get to my house against my better judgment, and I go back to sorting and cleaning my desk-stuff.

I finish my desktop and dress in my party outfit, which for me is a real change. I've decided to wear a hot pink ruffled skirt with an embroidered thin cotton blouse. When I look at myself in the mirror, I am reminded of the first day of school this year. It's like the old me is there with her eyes wide, gaping at this new person who parades in front of the mirror and wears hot pink ruffled skirts. I can almost see this mirage of myself waving goodbye and leaping into the emptiness inside the mirror. I wave back and hope Mom or Dad doesn't pass by my room.

Later, during the party when everyone is there and after the pizza, we hear the doorbell ring. A few minutes later, Maura makes her entrance.

"Oh, hi, everyone. Hi, Jen. Becky, Janie." She squeezes into the space on the sofa between Jennifer and Becky as if it has been held for her. "So what's going on? Did I miss much?" She laughs and clasps her hands in front of her.

I think she seems normal and relatively happy, maybe everything will be fine. After all it's been a long time since she's said anything nasty to me. So I want to believe she's not going to do that at my own party. I take a deep breath, and this time it's not so easy to breathe. I have a funny feeling all this might turn out horribly wrong.

"I have an idea." Maura interrupts our conversation like she's been talking all along.

"What is it? I know you always come up with something great. Do you remember the time we all had to hold an egg on a spoon while hopping up and down? I think it was at your twelfth birthday party." Jennifer giggles and adds, "Yeah, and remember what the floor looked like and how angry your Mom got?"

"I do, and I was lucky to get out of the house at all after that. She really hit the ceiling with that one. But I didn't care. We all had fun, right?" Maura looks like she's got one of those crazy ideas. Her eyes are shining, and she looks like she has the greatest secret. "How about if we liven up this party a little?"

"Um, okay, but no eggs on spoons." I'm starting to breathe a little bit faster. Is my party going to spiral out of control because of Maura?

"No, of course not. We're older now. How about if we play *Truth or Dare?*"

Everyone thinks this is a great idea, and after a little bit of deciding how we should do it and learning the rules, we start. I'm first, because it's my birthday and all. We're sitting in a big circle on the living room carpet and spinning an old diet soda bottle.

"Go ahead and spin it Carolyn, and whoever it lands on has to do what you say." Maura can be so bossy sometimes, like now.

The bottle spins and points toward Maura. I look her in the eyes and ask, "Truth or dare?"

Maura answers, "Truth."

I wrack my brain to figure out something I can ask her. Then it comes to me.

"Does your cousin really have chicken pox?"

Maura looks at me like I'd asked her to split herself in two. "What do you mean?

Didn't I tell you I couldn't go to her party?" Her voice goes up at the end, and she glares at me with her beady brown eyes.

"You don't have to get so angry, and why are you angry in the first place? Just tell the truth." I glare back at her and straight in her eyes. I wanted the truth, so she'd better answer.

Maura looks away finally, and then she looks back at me, and I know she's going to tell the truth. "Well, she did have the chicken pox, but that was about five years ago." She tries an offhand giggle, like she's so witty and cute, and it's okay to lie a little, right?

"So you didn't tell me the truth when you said you couldn't come. What is the truth here Maura?" My eyes are boring into her as if they can extract the truth.

When Maura answers this time, her voice has changed. Her face is moving into a snarl as she opens her mouth. "Did you really think I would come to your party? Do you want the truth, Carolyn? I've always thought you were a little nerd, and I wondered why Jennifer even bothered with you. Since she's been with you, she's not herself. She and I used to always hang out, and we had the coolest times." Maura pauses here and looks across at Jennifer.

Jennifer's face is composed. She never shows how she feels usually.

"And now everything's all twisted around. There's nowhere for me. I mean, Jen and I used to talk every day. She would tell me everything. Now I don't know what is going on in her life, and it's all because of you. You're the problem." Maura takes another breath, and I can see little tears beginning to form in the corners of her eyes. "You think you're so cool now you're a cheerleader, but you forget that only last year you were the 'breathe, Carolyn, breathe,' girl to us. You know why we bothered you? It was fun. You should have seen your face when we said it."

Becky, Janie, and even Jennifer come up behind me as Maura is speaking. Becky puts her hands on my shoulders and so does Janie. Jennifer comes and sits with the two of them.

"I can't believe I'm hearing this, Maura. Carolyn has been the best friend anyone could ever hope to find. Sure she can't dress, and I've had to show her how, but what she is inside is ten times better than how you are. And yes, you and I were friends once, but I've grown up, and you haven't. I feel sorry for you Maura."

Jennifer sits next to me, and it's us four facing Maura.

"So now you're standing up for your little friend, Carolyn. I'm surprised at you, Jen. I thought we were a team." Maura is really crying now.

"If being a mean, rotten person is what I have to do to be on your team, forget it. You know I actually asked Carolyn to invite you. She did it for me. I thought you and I were friends, but I guess I was wrong." Jennifer says with tears in her eyes.

"Look, guys. This is my birthday party. And as fun as this has been, I want everyone to have a good time. So can't we stop this? I'm glad I learned the truth, and hey, I know all about how Maura feels about me." I give the bottle to Maura to spin.

She dries her eyes with the back of her hand and soon the bottle is spinning again.

The bottle spins and arrives at Jennifer. Maura smiles. I'm not sure I like that smile at all.

"So, Jen, *truth or dare?*"

"I think *dare.*"

"Okay, I dare you to walk out of this party with me and never speak to this geek again." Maura gets up and starts to leave the room.

"I'm not doing that. I'm having fun. Anyway, we haven't had Carolyn's mom's chocolate chocolate chip cookies yet, and I don't want to miss those." She turns to me and says, "You know how I love those."

Maura stops as if frozen and stares at Jennifer. I'm glad it's not me getting that stare. It's like her eyes are weapons, and I feel as if Maura would like to pull the trigger and shoot Jennifer with her attack beams. But Jennifer just continues as if nothing is wrong. "Okay, my turn to spin the bottle." Jennifer spins the bottle, and it lands on herself. "*Truth or dare,* Maura. Which should I pick?"

Maura turns and comes back to the group. I don't even think she knows why she's there.

"You aren't coming with me are you? You'd rather stay at this little dweeb's house and play this stupid game." Maura's mouth is starting to turn down a little.

"What do you mean? Wasn't this game your idea? What's wrong Maura?"

As soon as Jennifer says this, a torrent of water comes from Maura's eyes. I didn't think eyes held that much water. "Jen…Jen…I, I, d…d…o…n't…know…why I'm doing this. Y, y…ou…are always with Carolyn lately and we n…n…e…v…e…r get any time to sp…sp…end with each other. I guess I'm jealous." Maura breaks down for real and sobs.

Becky, Janie, and I don't believe this. Can it be the suave and sophisticated Maura crying in front of us?

Jennifer goes up to Maura and puts her arms around her. She and Maura hug. Then Jennifer answers her own question. Jennifer picks truth, and to my amazement, she tells us the one thing I thought she would never tell. "Carolyn knows this and probably Becky and Janie, because they're Carolyn's friends, and now I think you should know it, too."

Maura looks puzzled. "What are you talking about, Jen?" She seems to have recovered her composure, and she dabs at her eyes with a tissue while she's talking.

"I'm talking about what happened to me in school when I fainted, and why I sometimes come to school like a ghost. Also, why I'm not able to see you so often, and why I fell off the balance beam."

Maura still looks uncertain about what Jennifer is saying. "I mean don't you wonder how I can stay so thin and still eat so much when we hang out? Have you ever thought about how many trips I take to the ladies' room wherever we are? Why do you think?"

Maura answers, "I don't know. I thought maybe you drank a lot of water and had to go a lot. Or maybe you do all those gymnastics, and you burn away the food."

"Sure that would work, but it's not the reason. Do you want to know the reason?"

Jennifer looks toward Maura with a question in her eyes.

"I guess, if you have to tell me. I don't spend much time thinking about all that, you know." Maura is still dabbing at her eyes with the tissue and gives her nose a loud blow.

"Carolyn guessed why a few times after we met, and I decided to let her know, because I was getting sick of doing it. You want to know, huh, why I keep this perfect body?"

Everyone in the room is waiting for Jennifer to tell us, even though, except for Maura, we know why. But we're caught up in the moment.

Jennifer continues, "The reason is…" She pauses a little bit, and I think there should be a drum roll. Then I see her eyes. Jennifer is scared. Once the words come out, there's no taking them back. There are no more excuses for anyone. I look at Jennifer, and she seems to be having trouble breathing.

"Are you okay, Jen? You don't have to tell her, you know. It's just a game," I say.

Janie and Becky add, "Yeah, Jennifer, we don't have to hear you say it. It'll be okay."

Then I look at Jennifer and realize she can't do it. She can't open her mouth. She starts to cry and motions to me to do it.

I look Maura straight in the eye and say, "The reason is…" And I hear that drum roll in my head when I say it, "Jennifer's bulimic. She's been that way since middle school."

Maura looks like she's been hit by a ten-ton truck.

"That's why I haven't been able to see you on Wednesday nights like we used to. I am in therapy three nights a week. Carolyn has known all about this, and it's because of her I had enough nerve to tell my parents." Jennifer puts her hands over her head and stretches. "Whew, I never knew how you felt when you have that breathing problem, Carolyn. That was scary. Thanks for helping me out. I honestly couldn't talk for a while. Wow, I'm sorry I ever teased you about the breathing thing."

I laugh. Then Maura comes over to Jennifer and hugs her. I go over and hug Jennifer too, and soon Becky and Janie join our circle. We're all crying and hugging each other in turn when Mom comes into the room.

"What's going on girls? Isn't this a birthday party?"

"Mom, it's nothing. We're playing this game. Can we have your cookies now?"

"Sure, I thought you'd never ask. Let's all go into the dining room. I have something for you." Mom walks in front of us, and we all go into the dining room arm in arm. As we're walking, we start talking.

"This is fun. You know when we were sitting together at lunch, I was always worried about being there because of you, Maura," I say. Then I get this great idea. It comes out of nowhere, and I'm not sure everyone will agree, but it's my party, and I figure why not try.

"Hey everybody, how about if we make a pact we'll all be friends next year?"

I'm looking around and waiting, when suddenly Becky shouts, "Great idea, Carolyn. Let's do it."

Then the five of us get in a circle and put our hands together in a crisscross.

"What'll we say?" Janie asks.

"Let's promise to always be there for each other. Just like Carolyn has always been there for us," Jennifer says. "I wish everyone could be like Carolyn Samuels." Jennifer smiles at me.

In front of me, my birthday cake with pink roses on white frosting with fifteen candles and one to grow on glows. Mom is smiling at me. Everything shifts into place. Looking at Mom and all my friends singing and grinning, I take a deep breath, make a wish, and blow out the candles. Making the first cut, I see it is chocolate cake. My favorite.

Max licks his lips and stares at the cake with his tongue hanging out until I have to give him a tiny piece. He looks up at me with grateful eyes. You know, you can learn a lot from Max. I used to wish my life were that simple, but it's not anymore. Max has a great time begging cookies from everyone, and finally he lies down on the tile floor in the kitchen like a giant black area rug.

That night, after chocolate birthday cake and Mom's amazing chocolate chocolate chip cookies, I think about what Jennifer said. All this time, I've wanted to be like Jennifer Taylor, and all along she's wanted to be like me. I look at my friends sleeping around me. Laying my head on the pillow, I close my eyes and smile. Next year waits for me like a birthday present. I can't wait to unwrap it.

About the Author

221

Barbara Ehrentreu is a retired teacher and the Regional Director for the West for Motivational Strips. She lives in Stamford, CT with her family. She has two published books and a poetry book and is in numerous international anthologies. She has won the coveted Indian Independence Day Honor from Gujarat Shaitya Academy and Motivational Strips for 2020, 2021 and 2022, Rabindranath Trigore Memorial Award from SIPAY magazine, Motivational Strips and the Seychelles government for 2022 and several other international awards for her writing. Recently she won 3rd prize in the Malaysian International Poetry Contest. She hosts a radio show, Books &Entertainment Tales from the Pages and is a member of Greenwich Pen Women Letters and SCBWI.

Who Is Jennifer Taylor?

Chapter 1

I did two perfect somersaults and a double twist in the air bouncing off the balance beam to stick the landing. As I stood there with my arms still in the air I glanced over to the bleachers. Carolyn didn't make it, but there was Brad with his phone aimed at me. I smiled at him as my coach came over to congratulate me.

"This is the best you've done all year, Jen, and I think with a little more practice you will be ready for next week's competition." He hugged me and I hugged him back. It had been a long way to this day and we both knew it.

This got me thinking about last year and where I had been in my head around this time. It was fall and I had been practicing all summer except for a few weeks when Mom had to make me leave and go to Florida. When I got back all I could think about was getting back to practice and of course that didn't happen. In fact, she had all these dinners planned for us to go to, and really if it weren't for Carolyn, I probably would not have gotten through the first part of school. She did my homework for me and that's when I saw she was not who I had thought she was.

What Carolyn did for me last year can't be told in one sentence. She really probably saved my life and helped me to have a better relationship with Brad. I wondered where she could be now. She said she'd be here to see me practice.

"Jen," I heard a familiar scream as I walked toward the bench. "I meant to be here. I really did, but cheerleading practice went on forever and so I'm here too late! Oh, I did see you on the balance beam, though. Brad sent the video, and I was watching it as I was running here from the field."

Carolyn ran up and hugged me. "I'm all sweaty from practice," I told her.

"I am too." Carolyn's face was all red. "I don't mind. I'm so happy for you and I just couldn't contain myself."

Carolyn laughed and I laughed too. We both looked up at the bleachers as we heard male laughter. "You girls crack me up. Last year all you did was bicker and moan about each other and now you're hugging."

"Weren't you around when we made up? I did tell you about this when Carolyn tried out for cheerleading practice, and did you forget how she filled in for me at Homecoming? I mean didn't you say you had a good time with her that night? Don't you remember?"

Brad smiled and said, "Sure I do. I was just kidding around with you guys."

I couldn't get up to the bleachers to smack him, but I raised my fist in the air and Brad just smiled back. He was so goofy sometimes.

"You know, Jen. What Brad said reminded me of how I used to feel about you right around this time last year."

"Yeah, I guess I was pretty rotten to you when we were first starting here."

"Well, you were pretty rotten to me all through middle school."

"Yeah, I know. But you have to remember what I was going through then, and to be honest it was Maura who egged me on and made me do a lot of it. I wanted to stop, but she kept telling me how much fun it was to see you when I sneaked up on you."

"Actually, I wondered how you did that."

"Well, Maura would scout out where you were and then text me so I'd know, and I could find you. Then it was easy."

"Diabolical, that's what you two are together!" Brad came toward us. We both laughed. That's where we were this year.

"So how was practice? Where's Maura? She said she'd come too."

"Oh, she had this guy who picked her up and she said she'd call you when she could."

"Uh, oh. I hope it wasn't Danny. Did he have blonde hair and a cute face?"

"Now that you mention it he was blonde and definitely cute."

"Girls," Brad shouted, "I have to get out on the field or my coach will nail me."

"Oh, sorry, honey. Come over here and give me a hug. I've got to ice my ankle before I can do anything."

Brad jumped over the railing and landed in front of me. I was always amazed at how high he could jump. He should really be in gymnastics.

"Here's a hug and something extra." He put his arms around me, gave me a kiss on the lips and ran his tongue over his own lips. "You're wearing that yummy lip gloss again." He headed toward the door of the gym. "I'll call you after practice. Maybe we'll do something tonight and definitely wear that lip gloss."

I smiled and blew him a kiss. He didn't see it because he had his back turned to me.

"You guys are so cute together," Carolyn said.

"Yeah, he's a great guy and he puts up with a lot from me."

"Oh, you're not too bad once someone gets to know you. Although now that I do know you, I'm not so sure I'd want your life." We both laughed at this one, because last year she really wanted to be just like me.

"Jen, here's your ice and you need to keep it on for at least ten minutes." My coach came over with the ice pack and a towel and he made me put up my ankle so he could wrap the ice around it.

"You don't have to stick around for this if you have something else to do." I looked over at Carolyn.

"No, Jen, I don't have to be home until late. It's dinner with my dad tonight and you know what that means."

"Yeah, either take out or go to a restaurant. Is he picking you up?"

"Yeah, but it's going to be around five thirty. What time is it now?"

We both looked up at the gym clock.

"It's five now. So, stay here and we'll talk some more."

"Sure."

"Hey, we never got a chance to talk about cheerleading camp. How was it?"

"It was incredible and very hard. Each day they asked us to do things I never thought I could do in a million years, and yet I did them. I mean my tumbling is just excellent now."

Carolyn ran over to the mat nearby and did three excellent somersaults in a row.

"Wow, you really did learn up there. How was everything else?"

"Well, there were no guys up there and anyway you know I'm still with John."

"Yeah, I know, because he and Brad kept pestering me about you. Seriously, John came up to me on the street and asked about you. Then Brad would ask me about you because John had pestered him. Didn't you guys talk at all?"

"No, we couldn't have any contact with the outside world. It was like a prison up there. I mean we could watch TV and had the internet and video games, but you can't make any phone calls at all. I guess they had an incident the year before when someone complained to their parents about how hard it was, and then they yanked her out of there.”

“Well, it was hard on me, because I couldn’t tell either of them about what was going on with you.”

“I don’t know. It wasn’t too bad being away from Mill Valley. My parents are so demanding sometimes that it was good to get away from them for a while.”

“I would love to get away from my parents.” I thought of how great it would be to be away from my mom and dad for a couple of weeks. Now that I had almost kicked this eating disorder my mom was everywhere making sure I didn’t start again. She checked my drawers and my closet and kept watch on when I went to the bathroom. It was like living in a prison in my own home.

“Yeah, I know what is going on with your situation and maybe your mom is right to be on you like that. I know you hate it, but hey, do you want to end up like you were last year?”

I thought of last year and how miserable I was. How I couldn’t stop myself from binging and purging until my accident brought me to my senses. I hadn’t thought about it much, except of course at therapy where I went three times a week and talked about pretty much everything.

The thought of having myself in that predicament again brought it all back to me, and suddenly I realized even though I was better, I could still fall back into my old ways. I grabbed Carolyn’s hand. “You know I don’t want that to happen again ever. I’ve been working so hard on keeping myself from my old ways, and you have always been a big help to me. You’re the best friend I’ve ever had.”

Carolyn’s eyes filled with tears and I felt mine tearing too. “Jen, I’ll always be there for you no matter what.”

I looked her in the eyes and though they were blurry I saw Carolyn’s beautiful brown eyes staring back at me with such kindness and care that I couldn’t hold myself together anymore. “I’m so afraid as this meet gets closer and closer that I’m going to crack. I really need you more than ever now. I'm trying to look strong to Brad and my parents, but I'm really scared.

This is my last chance and if I don't make it, I'll have no more time left. I'll be too old for the next Olympics."

Carolyn wrapped her arms around me, and the two of us stayed there in silence.

"It's time, Jen." My coach came over and Carolyn and I separated. You can go now, but please remember you're in training. So early to bed and no extra activities like dates or parties until after the meet. That's only a week and I think you can do it. Meanwhile, exercise that ankle as much as you can. Do the rehab exercises every day. We need that to be as limber as possible."

"Thanks, Coach. You know I'll have to follow what you say." I knew I would try, but not going out. That wasn't going to work at all. How could I not go out with Brad? But I would do anything to win this meet even if it meant giving up my social life. So, I would have to stay in this week. If that was what it took to win I could do it.

"It's almost five thirty. Why don't we go out and wait for your dad. My mom or dad is picking me up. I never know which one will be free."

"Yeah, great idea."

I started unwrapping my ankle and changed into my jogging pants throwing on my jacket. I changed my beam socks for regular ones and sneakers and grabbed my bag. "We're outta here," I said. I was glad to be getting out into the fresh air. The gym's odors were getting to me after a whole day of high school boys and girls.

We walked over to the gym's double doors and pushed them open. There was Maura standing in the hall with the cute blonde guy wrapped around her.

"Ahem," I cleared my throat.

Maura looked up and she looked a little frazzled, which is unusual for her. "Hey Jen and Carolyn. Umm, this is Danny."

"Hi," Danny said his face a little red as he extricated himself from Maura. "I don't think I know either of you girls."

"Yeah, well, you don't look familiar either. Unless you are the new guy in my history class."

Danny smiled and he really looked hot. I could see why Maura was all over him. But how long did they know each other?

"Yeah, you've got me. I just moved here and don't know too many people. But Maura lives right near me so we kind of met before school started."

So, Maura knew him before school and didn't tell me. I glared at her.

"Jen, I wanted to, but you were so busy with your practices and Brad and the other thing you do that we didn't have much time to talk. You know I just got back from Florida. My parents dragged me there this year and I had to miss cheerleading camp. Carolyn, you went. How was it?"

"Well since it was my first time, I have nothing to compare it with. We had lots of practice in the basics. I'm sure you didn't need it. I've seen you cheer and the people there were not as good as you."

"I know that's not true, but you're a sweetie to say that. Maura looked at Jennifer, "I see what you mean about her, Jen. She is something else."

"Yeah, she is kind of a gem."

Carolyn started blushing and said, "That's a little too much guys. I'm just trying to do the right thing."

"You're right. Sorry."

"So, are you guys an item or anything?" Jennifer asked Maura.

"Well, we have been going out for like two weeks, but I don't know."

Danny started sweating and bouncing on the balls of his feet. "You know guys I have to go, because I have an important thing to do right now." He practically ran down the hall.

"Was that too much for him? I guess we kind of stuck our foot in our mouth." I said.

"Speak for yourself, Jen. I think he was spooked by having to say anything. It's too much too soon. I don't think we have it figured out yet. Don't worry. It's not serious. You know me."

"I do know you and I also know you don't get involved. So, tell me the truth. Two weeks is a long time for you, Maura."

"Okay, I do kind of like him, but now I don't know what's going to happen."

"Oh, don't worry. I'll talk to him in History class and persuade him that we were just kidding around."

"Phew, if you do that, I'll do anything for you."

"Oh, don't say that, because last year I said that, and Jennifer made me do her homework for weeks." Carolyn said laughing.

I laughed too remembering how we managed that trick in the hallway when we exchanged loose leafs and papers. I knew then Carolyn was a really different kind of person than I had ever met.

Maura walked out of the school with us, and Carolyn ran over to her dad who was waiting there for her. "See you tomorrow," she said. Then she ran back and said, "Remember, if you need anything call me or call your therapist. I mean it." She squeezed my hand and waved goodbye to us as she got into the car.

"I really love that girl, you know. Who would think we would be BFF's this year."

"I know, Jen. It's crazy, but then it's been a crazy year."

Just then my mom drove up in her brand-new BMW and I got into the car waving at Maura and yelling out the window, promising I would call her too.

"So how was practice today, Jen?" Mom said as I got into the car and fastened my seatbelt.

"Oh, it was fantastic! I did it. I did two and a half somersaults on the balance beam and a double twist and stuck the landing. The coach says I'm ready for next week."

"I'm so proud of you, honey." My mom hugged me and then got out of the parking space.

"My coach says that I can't go out at night until next week." Why did I tell her that? I could have actually kept it from her, but the new Jennifer didn't want to lie anymore. I wanted to do the right thing and I wanted to keep myself from getting into my old habits. As I drove home, I said a little prayer to the Olympic gods that I could keep my promise.

www.ingramcontent.com/pod-product-compliance
Lightning Source LLC
Chambersburg PA
CBHW040526170726

48295CB00012B/350